THE

SCARECROW MAN

THE

SCARECROW MAN

Christopher Bray

NEW YORK   *The Viking Press*

For Jody

FIRST PUBLISHED IN 1968 BY THE VIKING PRESS, INC.
625 MADISON AVENUE, NEW YORK, N.Y. 10022

LIBRARY OF CONGRESS CATALOG CARD NUMBER: 68-29053

PRINTED IN U.S.A.

THE

SCARECROW MAN

I

Just when Gonlag was ready to drop below the pavement, negotiate the sewers and the electricity and gas and water mains and see if he could find Surzo, and just when he was taking a last look round, he saw the man walking towards him across the road.

The man walked slowly past the women standing by the taxis, and slowly past the hot-dog stalls and when he came to where Gonlag was sitting, he said, 'May I share your part of the wall?'

Gonlag was as surprised as ever by the man's politeness, and shifted himself a little, saying nothing.

The man sat down and coughed slightly and Gonlag asked him how he was.

'Oh, well, well,' he said absently, 'and how are you?'

'Never seen things brighter,' declared Gonlag, without any smile.

They settled back against the railings. Gonlag's companion turned his face up to the sky and he, Gonlag, set himself to thinking about Surzo again.

Same as last night, he thought resignedly, and the night before that. Soon as I drop down to visit Surzo, along comes this bloke, don't even know his name, and messes everything up.

Normally Gonlag would have told whoever it was to buzz off and leave a man in peace. But there was something about this one that puzzled him, he didn't know what. The man had an aura. And he allowed him to stay. As for visiting Surzo, that would have to wait.

Anyway, the last time he had seen Surzo, he'd had his eyebrows singed. 'You can tell dem from me, buster,' said Surzo in his coarse Brooklyn accent, 'you can tell dem from me I'm not taking much more. I'm for bustin' out and leavin' de joint but altogether!'

Just why he chose to speak in a Brooklyn accent Gonlag could never tell.

The way Surzo had spoken Gonlag had understood he was to communicate the information, and when he returned to the pavement, as it were, he had looked around for someone to tell. But he had seen no one who he thought would want to hear what Surzo had to say and had decided on some kind of a public announcement. He had been inspired to the idea of painting messages on walls here and there. Something like:

SURZO IS READY TO BUST OUT!
SURZO WON'T TAKE MUCH MORE!
BEWARE!
SURZO IS THE EARTH AND THE SPIRIT OF THE EARTH.
SURZO IS THE FIRE WITHIN THE EARTH AND HE KEEPS
MY FEET WARM AT NIGHT.

Something like that would do.

Gonlag was not one to whom a wall unwritten is no wall at all. He had only once, on a wall in a pub at Brighton, written anything. He wrote, 'I was here.' Since his inspiration, however, he had done nothing about it, lacking the opportunity and the materials. Paint, he had decided, was what was needed. Paint cost money. And now this bloke had come along out of nowhere and messed it up still more.

The man out of nowhere spoke.

2

'Look at that!' he said. He was still looking at the sky and Gonlag looked up to see. There was nothing up there out of the ordinary. The city threw up a barrier of light, lurid and unreal, so that the stars beyond were only visible here and there. Gonlag remembered seeing the moon above a flashing advertisement for Wrigley's Chewing Gum that evening and thinking how accidental it had looked in comparison.

'Can you see the stars?' the man asked.

'Only here and there,' said Gonlag.

'I thought so,' said the man. 'You see I used to wear glasses, until I lost them. I can't see so well now.'

'You want to try the National Health or the Portobello,' said Gonlag. 'One or the other.'

'Now if we were in the country, or at sea,' said the man, 'we would be able to see the stars very clearly. The city obscures the stars, just as it obscures all things natural. But it's a comfort to know the stars are still there, even if we can't see them.'

'I can see them,' said Gonlag. 'You want to get some glasses, like I said, from the Portobello or the National Health.'

'I know, I know,' said the man impatiently.

But the truth was that he liked the smudges and the blurs that his eyes gave him. The hard corners were rubbed off, or at least they wavered, and everywhere he looked he saw impressionistic muddles that melted and flickered and ran into each other. When he looked at the hot-dog stalls, his eyes put him one remove from reality, his myopia curbed his hunger, and for that he was grateful.

'I'll never get another pair of glasses,' he said.

Gonlag made no reply. He was thinking of the time he had been at sea and had gone one night as far as he could along the deck until he was pushing against the bow-

3

rail, with the sea cutting below him, and had looked along the curve of the horizon and everywhere seen the stars. He was not poetic. Stars were nothing more than stars to him, and nothing less, and if he'd been Keats when that bloke explained away the rainbow on a spectrum he would have said, 'So what!' and smiled like the bloody Sphinx.

Over the past years Gonlag had learned to live a very inward life. He upheld a rough exterior and his speech was coarse. Neither were his insides made of marshmallow. He had gone on learning and there were many places in his imagination he would never have found if he had spent his nights between two sheets and four walls. There was Surzo, for instance. He had discovered Surzo one winter's night four years ago when he had been stamping his feet hard on the pavement to keep them warm. It was then that the unmistakable accent had reached up to him.

As for the stars, he hadn't given them a thought for many a year.

'Listen,' said Gonlag, 'if you're thinking of making this regular you'd better give me something to call you by. My name's Gonlag.'

'Oh, I'm sorry,' said the man. 'My name's Mason.'

'Right then, pleased to meet you,' said Gonlag, suddenly awkward and wishing he hadn't said a word.

Mason, the man, laughed and coughed at the same time. Gonlag looked at him for a moment and then suddenly stood up on his feet as if he'd been bitten.

'You almost had me forgetting,' he said, 'I got enough papers for both of us tonight. Shivering won't get you warm.'

He opened his coat and drew out a great wad of newspapers and laid them on the parapet. When he pulled his coat together again he appeared much slimmer.

4

'Chap I know,' explained Gonlag casually. 'But first you've got to know about them. Most people think they're for reading, right?'

'Quite right,' said Mason, sure of his ground.

'Well,' said Gonlag, looking down at Mason from under his hat, 'most people are wrong, as usual. No! 'Course they've got news in them, but what's that? Here today and gone tomorrow! Now when I get a newspaper from somewhere I don't bother to read it. *Times* or *News of the World*, what does it matter, they all go under my coat for a warm-up and then up my shirt and down my trousers. Social security blankets they are, vermin free, and that's more than I can say for some of the hostels. Then again,' Gonlag was warming to his theme, 'what do you do when it's raining in the daytime? Go to the nearest Library, into the Reading Room, take *The Times* from the rack and sit by the radiator all day. Make out you're pondering the implications of somebody's speech to the Commons. With your eyes closed. Got the idea?'

'I think so,' said Mason.

'Newspapers!' said Gonlag. 'What marvellous things they are. Whenever I go down Fleet Street I say a little prayer.'

Gonlag suddenly stiffened, bringing his boots together with a bang and his arm up into rigid salute.

'God Bless Things The Way They Are!' he shouted.

As it was way past midnight there was nobody to take any notice. A policeman standing on the corner of the Edgware Road cocked his head, like a blue heron, and then began to impel his feet in an easterly direction down Oxford Street. At one-thirty-two a.m. proceeded in an easterly direction down Oxford Street.

The only other people who might have heard, apart from the shadows along the parapet, were four hot dog-stall

5

attendants, with two stalls between them, and three black taxis with the appropriate number of drivers, and several women hanging about for a pick-up.

When Gonlag shouted, all of these went on as if they were deaf. Mason was disappointed. He had expected some kind of reaction. He himself had jumped nervously, and he had liked the shout that had made him jump in the middle of the night with the wind blowing up his trouser legs and the policeman rocking away down Oxford Street as if a Sergeant-Major had ordered an about turn.

One of the women watched the policeman walking away, and the nearest hot-dog man, after a pause, turned balefully in the direction of the shout and then back again, spitting on the pavement and saying viciously, 'The only Father Christmas I ever fuckin' saw was one they get down Woolworths every year,' the breath spurting white from his lips. The rest was inaudible.

But Gonlag had already dropped his hand and said, 'What are you thinking about, sitting there then?'

'Nothing much,' Mason replied.

'Well then,' said Gonlag, 'fish and chips, don't forget fish and chips. And lighting fires.' And he began tucking some newspapers down his trousers and under his shirt. 'Help yourself,' he said, 'there's plenty. And don't forget your bum. These cold nights.'

Mason stood up and did as he was told. When they both sat down again they crackled softly.

'Thanks,' said Mason.

A policeman paced by like a shark from the depths and Mason huddled deeper into his coat. When he was out of earshot Gonlag said, 'It's not my nature to be inquisitive, but if you've done something, and I'm not saying you have, that's the way to make them spot you.'

Mason thought for a moment and then said, 'You're

quite right, Gonlag. Next time I'll look him in the eye and say "Good Evening".'

'Oh, Gord!' said Gonlag theatrically. 'Next time he comes past he'll tell us to move on, you wait and see.'

But neither of them believed it. There was something too stable about the night for anything like that. The newspapers insulated them against the cold and they knew a measure of comfort.

Everybody's different. Some people it's cars, some it's women, most dogs it's lamp posts, and for Gonlag and Mason and their kind it was places to spend the night. They chose Marble Arch separately but for the same reason. There was always something going on. It was like being in the theatre. Behind them there was nothing but the railings against which they leant and Hyde Park. Everything, all that was of the city, was in front. Food from the hot-dog stalls and from the women warmth and sex. That's what turned it into a theatre. They only had the price of admission. Then there was the Law, of course, and the now occasional car that went round and round the Marble Arch and shot off down one of the roads like a stone from a sling. And best of all the men who appeared out of nowhere, seeming absent-minded but making straight for the taxis and the women and making off with both.

If the wind was blowing right they could smell it all at once: the hot dogs, the onions, the cigarette smoke, the women, and the taxi exhaust when one of them was lucky. And behind it all was the smell of the city, like some great and gaunt olfactory backdrop. The women, the stalls, and the taxis, even the policemen, became the night secretions of the city, and the whole of that fabricated immensity became nothing more, it seemed, than this shabby unit of commerce before them, multiplied a million times, and edi-

7

fied, sanctified, glorified above all, housed. The more pretentious the house the more illusive the illusion.

So sitting there the night through, Gonlag and Mason began to see things the way they are and smell the sum of seven million times hunger in the dry dead breath of the city, a concrete tomb laid upon the earth.

Next time I see Surzo, thought Gonlag, I'll ask him what he thinks about it all. He'll probably belch fire and stab his cigar at the air and say, 'De bums wanna remember who I am and what I is.' Gonlag pondered the words he had found. You don't find wisdom for sale in the market place, he knew that, and perhaps you don't have to go to the middle of the earth for it either, but he went there sometimes. There was a time when he had been afraid and he had approached a stranger or a friend with an adaptable crease in the corners of his eyes. But he had changed. One day he had spat on the floor of his soul and taken a broom to sweep it clean and said to himself, 'Right!' wiping his hands on his trousers. 'Right! That's it! Now I'll take on all comers. I'll nevermore lie with my eye or my tongue. When a stranger or a friend approaches I'll look them with a steady look that only wants to know them as they are, and no bossy bastard will ever come it over me again because of the way my eyes shine in misplaced humanity.' Gonlag had taken to the road. It was the best way he knew of expressing himself. It was very simple.

The women, the hot-dog men, the taxi drivers, the isolated policeman who dragged words in long balloons of frosted breath from the stall-keepers when he passed that way, that was the night world, the microcosm. If anyone talked, the breath stood out from them like icicles or cigarette smoke and when one breathed out and smacked his hands together and said, 'Brrrrr!' the white breath spurted out and as it passed the traffic lights turned green perhaps,

8

or red or amber, before its momentum was lost and its quality dissipated, and the traffic lights continued, chameleon-like, to command a phantom traffic.

Gonlag and Mason looked out at this night world from under the brims of their hats and thought sometimes of the morning when the sun comes up and the alarm clocks alarm and there is a grovelling or a hop-skipping out of bed and into the cold streets and off. Somewhere. It gave them the talent, for which they spent many a cold night, for seeing the individual behind everything. They could see the Prime Minister sitting on the lavatory thinking of his holidays and the lavatory attendant sitting on the beach thinking of home. When they walked past a church they saw a priest in a black cassock squinting over the empty pews into the shadows, face white like a marble tomb, doubting. But it wasn't just that. It was more. Possessing it, they were unable to judge.

Yet in spite of it all there were many times during the night when they both wished they had money. Money to leave the theatre seats and climb up on to the boards, bite deep into a couple of hot dogs with a good dollop of browned and slimy onions, then walk, knowing exactly where, towards the best of the women and the dark unreal world of the back seat of a taxi.

What they experienced, and it had a strongly bracing effect, was the elemental thing. Between them and the others out there, there was a divide drawn, and the policeman patrolled it. They could not pay, that was it. But it made no difference, because they knew, sitting there, that in the end no one can pay, and they were lucky not to be able to make even a beginning. The knowledge held the comfort of a lucky sixpence lost deep in a trouser pocket.

Though they didn't always see it that way when the wind blew up their trouser legs and attacked liver and

9

lights, and one of the women smiled at a hot dog man and pulled her warm coat around her tight-looking hips.

'My God!' said Mason. 'I'm glad I haven't got my glasses any more.'

The less sharply he saw the sausages in the pan and the onions jumping and a woman's hip curve, the less keenly did his hunger stab him in the guts. Yes, he thought, and the less my hunger crawls, the less likely I am to get in a state and work up a sense of injustice and spoil the whole night and everything else.

That was a reason why he found himself liking Gonlag. He couldn't imagine him caring too much about anything to disturb his own centre. He would look, keen-eyed, and spit contemptuously. He didn't have a tooth in his head, though he couldn't be out of his thirties, and he didn't mind a bit why he, Mason, chose to spend the night sitting by his side. The first night they had met, Gonlag had looked at him quickly and with no trace of a welcome or of distance either in his eyes, and that he had liked. And for the first night since the winter began he was more or less warm, thanks to the newspapers.

Mason coughed quietly, remembering the cold nights.

He looked at Gonlag. His head was dug deep into his coat with just his eyebrows protruding above the collar. He wore an old hat which he pulled down over his ears and his breath steamed up and around them and the wavy brim of his hat and away into the night. Just seeing him sitting there was good, a steady witness to the night, making his peace with the way things are.

So the night passed softly on the caterpillar feet of hunger.

It was concluded, not by the rising of the sun, for it was winter, but by the withdrawal of the players on the stage. The hot-dog men slammed shut the lids of their stalls, called to each other in abrupt courtesy, tucked the wooden shafts under their arms and trundled away, rumbling on iron-shod wheels in their different ways into a street-lamp dawn. The women and the taxis dissolved into puffs of exhaust and the policeman too seemed to find his presence no longer necessary and exited in his own solemn way. Along the stone parapet the huddled figures stretched and scratched and fumbled and slowly allowed the recognition of another day into their numbed senses.

When Gonlag had watched the taxis disappear he said, 'Here's a fact. Every twenty-eight minutes of the day somebody's sexually assaulted.' He spoke as if it were a trump card.

Mason didn't know what to say.

'Where?' he asked. Gonlag seemed to be expecting some response.

'In the United States of America! In Mummy's Own Country!' Gonlag told him.

Mason was surprised.

'How do you know?' he asked.

It was what Gonlag had been waiting for. With a flourish he dived a hand under his coat, drew out a crumpled newspaper and waved it above his head.

'In here!' he cried. 'In here!'

Mason was impressed, and he realized, gratefully, that here was someone to whom he could talk about the Scare-crow Man. It was the flourish that did it. The flourish and the matching fact, and the definite avowal that newspapers were printed blankets and nothing more. The incongruity appealed.

2

When at last the Underground gates rattled open Gonlag and Mason crossed the road and walked down the steps to the ticket office where a green-faced man gave them tickets to Covent Garden.

Almost against his own will Gonlag had told Mason about Covent Garden and asked him if he would like to come with him that morning. Gonlag was a solitary man yet he had asked for company.

When they surfaced again Gonlag sniffed the air appreciatively as he always did. It was full of the sweet and sour of fruit and vegetables and flowers. He led the way past the back of the Opera House towards a scene of absorbed activity. Lorries were loaded and unloaded, carts stacked and trundled, the fruit, flowers and vegetables passed from hand to hand, curving through the air, piled high on porters' heads, all done with a speed and casual precision approaching madness. Behind it all the human ants, talking and tattling, lifting, lugging, pushing, pulling and sweating. Here and there, unavoidably, an orange, a pear, or an onion, tumbled off a load and fell to the pavement.

Gonlag and Mason wandered through the halls of the Market and along the pavements, picking up whatever they fancied from the gutters and pavements, and putting it in their pockets.

When their pockets were bulging and they thought they

had enough food for the day and had begun to straighten their backs and pat their pockets smilingly, they saw on the ground in front of them a small hessian sack. Gonlag stopped and his eyes lit up. He picked it up, saw it had no holes, and said, 'It's near Christmas, isn't it? We need a bit of money.'

He bit his lip. He had said 'we', his mouth had said it, and he wondered, but he went on speaking. 'This could be useful! What we'll do, we'll fill it with the best fruit and vegetables we can find. I'll see to the rest of it.'

The sack too, they nearly filled in the same way as their pockets. Then Gonlag said, 'Good! We've got enough! Let's get a cup of tea.'

But Mason stood his ground.

'What's up?' asked Gonlag.

'I haven't enough money for tea, and I can't have you pay for me. You already paid my fare here.'

'Think nothing of it,' said Gonlag, 'if you had the dough you'd do the same for me, so come on. I'm cold and I'm thirsty and I've been dreaming about this cup of tea all night.'

He walked off. Mason watched him go. When he had gone twenty paces he turned and faced Mason again. He spread out his arms, lifted his head, and said, 'Pretend it's a gift from Heaven,' and walked on again, reached the café and disappeared.

Mason stood staring after him. 'If I hadn't known it was Gonlag,' he said to a pigeon that pecked a flattened banana at his feet, 'I'd have said it was the Scarecrow Man come to the city.'

Presently he followed Gonlag to the café, lugging the sack of fruit and vegetables over his shoulder.

When he opened the café door Gonlag had to wave to him and call his name before Mason saw him.

13

'Oh, there you are!' he said, sitting heavily in a chair and dumping the sack just as heavily beside him.

Gonlag winced. Then he pushed towards him a cup of tea and a white plate with a slice of white bread upon it that had the appearance of being camouflaged. 'Go for your life,' he said. 'It's muck, but there, I like it,' he said after a pause, and then he put the cup to his lips and sucked the hot tea audibly between his gums.

Mason asked him why he didn't invest in a pair of false teeth, for the noise Gonlag made could be heard throughout the entire café, though it was not large. Several heads turned their way and the woman behind the counter shrugged and then leered at one of her familiars.

'You should hear me with pea soup,' said Gonlag cheerfully. He put down his cup, looked round at the woman, and said, 'Morning, love.' She started and looked down her chin, wiping her hands hastily on a tea cloth. 'No,' he went on, 'I used to have a lovely set but I gave them to a pal of mine who wanted them for his honeymoon.'

They finished their teas and bread and butter. It was warm inside the café and they lingered there, lounging back in the chairs and toying with the tea cups.

'Back there,' said Mason, 'when you held your arms out, it was just like the Scarecrow Man.'

Gonlag digested this and said evenly, 'I suppose I do look like one sometimes.'

'No, no!' said Mason, 'perhaps I'll tell you tonight. Will you be there?'

'I'm always there,' said Gonlag, 'never fail.'

Mason seemed to be pondering something. He stared fixedly at a stain under the plastic table cloth. Suddenly he stood up and without saying a word to Gonlag, tripped over the sack and stumbled out of the door.

Gonlag caught him up at the corner of the road. It was

a damp chill morning, and the light was only just beginning to filter into the city. The street-lamps had recently gone out in sputtering orange glows. Mason was surprised to see him.

'Don't you want to be in on this?' said Gonlag, swinging the lumpy sack, for want of something better to say.

'It's all yours,' said Mason, 'but I'll help you collect them in the morning.'

They stood near the Underground and Gonlag suggested a breakfast below ground, on a bench on one of the platforms.

It was a good idea. Despite himself he wanted to find out more about Mason. Every man on the road, sleeping rough, had his reason, but there was something that irritated and intrigued about this one, and having given his company, Gonlag did not care to have it lightly set aside.

Mason however was unconscious of anything at that moment but the sudden chill in his bones and the rushing warmth of the Underground was very welcome. He was touched by Gonlag's patience with him.

Down below, in the Underground, they breakfasted off oranges, bananas and an apple or two. Then they surfaced again and went their different ways. But Gonlag, full of curiosity and apprehension, found himself trailing Mason through the streets, thinking to himself that he could do his selling later. The sack became heavy and Gonlag spat hard on the pavement. He watched while Mason stopped in front of a shop window full of Christmas decorations and stared at them muttering and shaking his head, before walking on. Mason was obviously new to the road and Gonlag wanted to help him where he could. It was always hard at first.

Not until Mason had led him through the stout iron gates of the British Museum did he realize where they were going. He watched him involve himself in the revolving doors, and whirl out of sight.

When Gonlag went in he got his sack caught, pulling himself free with such vigour that he bounced away across the floor.

A man in a blue uniform and cap stepped forward and announced himself.

'I'm sorry, sir,' he began.

'I know,' said Gonlag, smiling a dangerous smile, 'it's all right, Sergeant-Major. Which way did he go, did you see?'

For there was no sign of Mason.

'I'm sorry, sir,' said the man again. He looked like a chauffeur. There were several standing by, hands behind backs, teetering and looking approachable. 'I'm sorry, but you can't bring that in here, sir.' He seemed to relish this kind of impersonal courtesy.

'Well, would you take care of it while I look for my friend?' asked Gonlag. No sign of Mason still, he thought, and this is a large place. 'Are you sure you didn't see Mason? Dressed like me, same regiment, same age, no glasses, but got most of his teeth?'

The man took a step backwards, withering into ultimate impersonality.

'You *may* leave your sack with me, sir. I shall look after it. Your friend went that way. I happened to notice.'

The man took the sack and Gonlag followed where he had pointed. He couldn't have said what treasures he passed but for over half an hour he walked rapidly here and there, causing a small sensation among sightseers rooted before urns and mummies and statues. They watched his ragged hatted figure out of sight and turned again to art.

At last he found himself in a stone backwater, as it were, devoted solely to the Elgin Marbles, and standing before

16

a group of stone figures and already on the point of giving up the search for Mason he experienced the kind of hallucination sometimes experienced by the undernourished.

One of the statues spoke to him, by name.

'Psst! Gonlag! Over here!'

The voice was Mason's.

Gonlag whirled in the direction of the voice and saw half a hat and one eye protruding from the bottom right-hand corner of one of the stone groups. This particular group had scaffolding erected lightly over it and one or two of the figures were covered with dust sheets.

'There's room for you too!' said Mason.

'What?' said Gonlag. 'Behind there?'

He would have said more but he heard movement and turned to see a group of Scandinavian students nosing out the room, circling the walls and statues. They were all blue macs and fair hair. They had come in quietly and some of them had seen him talk.

Mason hadn't yet heard. 'Come on,' he said, 'I can't move, I've got the cramp.'

'Shut up!' hissed Gonlag. 'People!'

Mason popped his head back behind the statue and said no more, but a group of students moved irresistibly towards Gonlag, saying Scandinavian things to each other and grinning.

Gonlag didn't know whether to pretend to have fleas, fart, or throw a fit. 'Now you've done it,' he muttered at the statue.

At that moment a man in uniform stepped into the room, hands flapping behind him vacantly and Gonlag decided to leave Mason to his fate for a while and move to the exit. But the group of students followed him so he darted quickly outside and hid noticeably behind a public notice board and when they passed him he jumped out on them with

17

a resounding belch. The group scattered, the girls giggled, and Gonlag went back inside again. They followed him no more.

When the students left the uniformed man followed them, his head on one side and a light in his eye from watching the girls' legs.

All was clear again.

'Mason!' Gonlag called. Mason's head popped out. 'Why don't you come out here, damn you!'

'I'm not moving,' said Mason. 'Why should I?'

So Gonlag climbed under one of the scaffold pipes, dodged another, lifted a dust sheet and discovered Mason sitting upright behind the statue like a crumpled statue himself.

'Where's the sack?' Mason asked at once.

'Never mind the sack,' said Gonlag. 'What on earth are you doing here?'

Mason pricked up his ears and whispered, 'Keep your voice down, I think someone just came in.'

Gonlag lifted the dust sheet and peered round the corner. An American woman was sizing up the Elgin Marbles. He nodded to Mason.

'How did you find me?' whispered Mason.

'Followed my nose,' said Gonlag.

Mason made no answer. Footsteps sounded, coming towards them. He winked. He opened his mouth and said in his deepest, most hollow, bass voice, 'Go home!'

They heard a gasp, a clatter and, after a pause, a recession of clip-clop footsteps.

'Here!' said Gonlag, 'I'm off! You're asking for trouble. Why did you come here in the first place. I mean, of all the places you could have chosen you choose this one.' Gonlag shook his head.

'I simply wanted a good kip.'

'What about the flicks then or the library?' asked Gonlag, his professional theories disturbed.

'No money,' said Mason, 'and I don't want company.'

Gonlag nodded then. 'Forgot about the money. See you tonight then. I'm off before that woman comes back with the Greek Prime Minister.'

He peered around the dust sheet cautiously and crawled out. When he was clear he called out 'Cheerio!' but there was no reply and he fancied he already heard a sibilant snore.

Gonlag left the Elgin Marbles shaking his head. But what could he do?

When he came to the main entrance again the uniformed man saw him coming and led him quietly to a cubby-hole where his sack had been stored.

'Did you find him?' asked the man.

'Yes,' said Gonlag. 'No, that is. Not really.'

The man scratched his head, pushing back his cap the way he had seen them do it in the films. It was also a natural gesture.

'I suppose you know best about that,' he said.

Gonlag's heart was lightened by the man's acceptance of things as they came to him and he forgot about Mason.

'Matey,' he said, 'your blood's worth bottling. Cheerio!'

'Cheerio,' said the man, 'and a Happy Christmas!'

'Oh, yes,' said Gonlag, 'and the same to you!' He picked up the sack, slung it over his shoulder, engaged the revolving door in an old-fashioned tango and nearly fell down the steps he was so happy.

'Steady,' he said to himself, 'steady. Mustn't get too lightheaded!' But remembering Mason sitting with his hat on behind a statue and the uniformed man pushing back his cap and scratching his head and all inside a place that looked like Buckingham Palace, well, it was too much and

19

he gave way to a surging feeling of goodwill that the cold wind and all the Christmas decorations in the world couldn't destroy.

'It must be my day,' he said aloud and at once wished he hadn't because the cold wind had got in at his gums.

He wanted to make more money. That was the first thing he wanted. And when he'd got the money he wanted to buy two things. The first was a bottle of red wine and the second was a hot dog with onions. If he had any money over he'd buy Mason one. He looked as if he needed a solid meal. With that cough of his. If he ever got out of the Museum again that was. And as for one of the taxi women, Gonlag's heart raced and his bowels leapt, as for one of the women . . . Then he caught himself and said with a hiss between his gums, 'Don't be a fool, man!'

All he had to do was to sell the stuff in the sack and to do that he had to get his foot in the right door. It wouldn't be easy, but money never did come easily, judging by the antics they got up to to lay their hands on the stuff. Jumping out of bed in alarm, rush hour, clothes, offices, bosses, always bosses. And the rest. The hell with it, thought Gonlag, I always manage somehow!

He counted his money, caught a bus at the beginning of Oxford Street and got off at Notting Hill Gate. He walked down Church Street and turned off to the left where his nose told him the money lived. His nose told him wrong. He tried house after house, flat after flat, but never got his foot beyond any door. He put his foot over one threshold and an old lady wearing blue hair kicked his ankle for him.

It was past midday, the wind was blowing grey geese from sick clouds, he was hungry, and he was still happy, when he saw outside a drab block of flats a van, a decorator's trade sign, two ladders, three brushes, and several tins of paint. This treasure was naturally not left

20

unguarded and two white-overalled men stood in the lee of the van, hopping from one foot to another.

When he saw all this Gonlag halted. His heart beat faster, and he knew it, all at once. HE WAS WHERE HE OUGHT TO BE ! His first thought then was to consult Surzo. He dropped the sack gently to the pavement and searched about for the biggest crack between the stones he could find.

'Are you there, Surzo?' he called. There was no time to go down and visit him.

'You ever know me when I ain't,' came Surzo's prompt and aggressive reply. Gonlag could see the sparks blowing up through the pavement from Surzo's cigar.

'I think I'm on to something,' said Gonlag. 'I've got this feeling.'

'Hang on to it, buster,' said Surzo, 'and don't let nuttin' stop yer. Go right ahead! And doze pots of crummy paint and de brushes, what do dey mean to you, huh?'

Surzo's accent was strong today.

'It looks as if the house is going to be painted,' said Gonlag.

A volcanic anger issued up from under the pavement and Surzo seemed to be struggling for words.

Gonlag thought again. 'I know what you mean,' he said at last, unmoved. 'O.K. I'll do it if I can.'

He heard a sigh of exasperation relieved, and just then the older of the two decorating men spoke to him.

'You all right, mate?'

'Just one of my turns,' said Gonlag.

The man seemed far from satisfied and he looked at his mate and his mate looked at him, but before they could say any more, Gonlag dragged the sack towards them, fumbled in his pocket, brought out a cigarette butt and asked them for a light. All of a sudden he was excited and he wanted just a few drags to think about the whole thing.

21

The men in turn fumbled in their pockets and produced both cigarettes and matches, standing their ground and keeping their eyes on Gonlag. 'Have one of these,' said the younger one, 'they're longer.'

'No, thanks,' said Gonlag, 'just the light. I roll my own, in my pocket.'

The cigarettes were lit and they concentrated, the three of them, on the first draw. The older man snorted the smoke down his nostrils, spat something from his lip and said, 'Thought you'd taken a turn back there.'

'Think nothing of it,' said Gonlag. 'I was communing.'

'Oh, yes,' said the man, and they both looked at him warily.

A car passed. A woman pushed a pram down the pavement towards them and when she had passed, the younger man said, 'I wish Father Christmas would wrap something like that up for me and put it in my stocking.' And he went, 'Corr!' in a good imitation of lust.

'Wouldn't know what to do with it if he did,' said the older man. 'Anyway she's married. Ain't you got no morals?'

The younger man cackled and stamped his feet, blew out cigarette smoke in the other's face and said, 'That's all you know. You ought to have seen that play on Telly last night, when that bloke. . .'

'Right,' said Gonlag. 'Thanks for the light.'

They watched him pick up the sack again, jog up the steps, try the main door, and disappear inside. Then the older man said, 'O.K. then. Let's do a bit.'

It was one of those houses that abound everywhere in London. Especially around Kensington and Notting Hill Gate, houses which had formerly given shelter to but one family and its servants and which now had every nook and cranny filled with a bed and perhaps a washbasin, where

22

lived a vast assortment of people unaware of each other's existence, where doors shut mysteriously, where lavatory chains were pulled and feet scuffled and heads popped out, where music seeped through the walls and luggage bumped on stairs, and laughter rarely came and sunlight yet more rarely, and where always a man sang Gilbert and Sullivan on the stairs, in the bath, on the lavatory and probably in his sleep too.

Nevertheless the street outside was lined with blackened cherry trees which flowered in the spring and haunted, inarticulate, in the winter. It was the cherry trees that had urged Gonlag on. He just couldn't believe they were alive and would flower again. And then the decorator's van had halted him and he had KNOWN.

He knocked at the first door he came to. Any door is much the same as another. It was the first door on the left. He trod his cigarette out on the floor and waited. The door opened.

Gonlag took off his hat, bowed slightly, and straightened up again, bringing a tight-gummed smile up from his boots. He saw a woman, perhaps in her thirties.

'Good afternoon,' he said, 'lucky to find you in. I was up before the birds this morning gathering these vegetables and choice fruits for you from the busy pastures of Covent Garden. In this sack I have your shopping problems solved.' He spoke without a pause, frankly amazed at the words that came from his lips. He felt he could do no wrong.

The woman smiled.

'Let me put the proposition to you now. Allow me to come in and you can judge for yourself the quality of the produce. Your Christmas shopping solved, your vitamins, your minerals, everything, ready here for your pleasure.'

'Well, I really don't know,' said the woman, toying with her ear. But she didn't shut the door.

'I'll tell you how I arrived here,' Gonlag went on, licking his lips, 'just to show you how strange are the workings of fate. After the harvesting at Covent Garden and a frugal breakfast at a popular Underground cafe I strolled with a friend to the British Museum itself, no less, where my friend had some business to attend to. I left him and caught a bus to this district where, after consulting Surzo, I knew I could do no wrong. And that's how you find me here,' said Gonlag finally. 'On your doorstep. Isn't that a strange history?'

He thought when he said 'on your doorstep' so strongly, she might have taken the hint but she just stood holding the door and said, 'It certainly is.'

'Is that coffee I smell?' asked Gonlag.

'Yes,' said the woman. She was smiling and slightly puzzled. 'Come in and have some anyway and I'll have a look at what you've got in the sack. It looks flipping heavy.'

She held the door aside for him and he slung the sack after him and put it behind the door. 'Now,' she said, smoothing the skirt down over her thighs, 'there we are. Sit down over there, if you like, near the fire. Do you take milk and sugar? Yes?'

'Anything you like,' said Gonlag, 'I'm easy.'

The room was small and warm, with a feminine feeling to it, yet the feeling didn't centre on any particular object. A gas fire hissed in the grate with a small mirror suspended above it, there was a double bed in the corner near the window with a blue counterpane upon it, the armchair in which Gonlag was sitting, and a kitchen recess and washbasin.

'Quite nice,' said Gonlag, nodding.

'What's that?' asked the woman, from the kitchen.

'All this,' he said, sweeping an overcoated arm. 'Would you mind if I took my coat off. It's warm in here and it's not the cleanest, my coat, and this is a good armchair.'

'Oh, bless you,' she said, 'don't bother yourself about that, but do take it off if you like. Coffee's nearly ready.'

Gonlag eased himself out of the chair and hung his coat behind the door. When he turned round the woman was putting two steaming mugs on the table.

'Wouldn't you like the chair?' he asked.

'No, no, no, you sit there. I'm all right here,' she said, perching on the edge of the bed. She caught up her mug of coffee and took two cautious sips. She smiled and said, 'That's better.'

Gonlag drank the coffee as slowly as he could. The woman brought out cigarettes and they lit them from the fire. She didn't want to talk very much and Gonlag liked that.

'Home comforts,' he said, grinning around him and to hell with his gummy mouth.

The woman smiled, sipped her coffee, flicked the ash from her cigarette and waved a hand as if brushing all nonsense aside.

'Let's have a look at the sack,' she said.

'Put some newspapers on the table then and I'll empty them out on there,' said Gonlag, who was glad to be getting down to business. He hummed a little to himself. This could be it, he thought, this could be it! A bottle of wine, hot dogs . . .

'One day,' he said, bursting out happily, 'if we get acquainted, I'll tell you about Surzo.'

The woman threw him an incendiary smile. She hadn't heard what he said. Her eyes were on the sack, which he upended carefully on the table.

'My!' she said. 'What a harvest!'

'Yours for the asking,' said Gonlag grandly.

'At a price,' she said.

'Well, if you could call it that,' he said. 'Sort out what

25

you want and we'll reckon it up. Remember the vitamins for winter!'

The woman sorted out four oranges, one grapefruit, three apples, five onions, eleven potatoes, and a battered cabbage. 'Pity you've no carrots,' she said.

'Yes,' said Gonlag. 'How about six bob the lot?'

'Make it five and my money's yours,' she said, with battle in her eye.

Gonlag looked deeply grieved. 'All right then,' he said, 'five and six, there you are.'

The woman at once fetched her purse and put two half crowns and a sixpenny piece in his grubby palm.

He began to laugh then because he had played his part, and then the woman laughed too because it was the first time she had ever pulled a bargain and said the right words or even troubled to disagree. She was exhilarated. She had fought a tiny battle to a draw.

'A draw is best,' she said, 'there should be no victories.'

'You're right,' said Gonlag, 'not between people.'

Her eyes were warm. They didn't bother to twinkle and crinkle. They lived.

'What about the rest of the stuff?' she said.

'I'll take it away, won't I. You don't want it,' said Gonlag.

It was time for him to go and he moved to the door.

'Would you like another cup of coffee before you go? I know it's cold outside,' she said.

So they sat down again and she put the full mugs of coffee between the fruit and vegetables on the table.

'It's sugared,' she told him. 'Do you live round here?'

'I suppose I do. Marble Arch mostly anyway. I sleep rough.' Gonlag watched for her reaction.

'What!' she said. 'You mean you haven't got a home?'

'That's right,' he said. 'That's the way I like it.'

26

She shivered and looked at him critically. 'You look well on it,' she said.

'I look after myself. Live on the fat of the land,' he said, 'but I'm saving up to buy a hamburger.'

She laughed and slapped her leg at that. But Gonlag sat with a straight face and she laughed the more. She had most of her teeth, with a gap between the two in the front.

'It's not fair,' he said, 'you've got a mouthful and I've got none.'

She shut her mouth. 'That's your fault,' she said.

Gonlag thought to himself, yes, it's just possible, I'll give it a go. He cleared his throat.

'Look,' he said, 'you've been good to me. Do you think I could have a bath? I never like to let Christmas go without one. I wouldn't ask normally but I like you. I can pay for it. Got the money now!' He patted his pocket half-heartedly.

She said nothing for a while, thinking it out. Presently she said, 'Would you like it now?'

Gonlag nodded.

'Just a minute,' she said, 'wait here and I'll see if anyone's in there.' She left the room quickly, skipped up a short flight of stairs, opened a door, shut it, and came down again. She was quite excited and almost whispered to him, 'It's all right, there's no one in there!' She gave him a towel, and a bar of soap, and ushered him out of the room and up to the bathroom like a hospital matron.

'Have a good soak,' she said, and closed the door.

The hot water tap gave forth hot water and the cold water tap cold. The bath plug fitted. There was nothing more to be desired. When it was filled Gonlag settled back until his chin rested just above the water.

'That silly bastard Mason,' he said, and chuckled.

He breathed a deep sigh.

27

3

When Gonlag left and the dust sheet fell back behind him and he called 'Goodbye', Mason was already settling back for a sleep. There was room enough for him to stretch out without either his head or his feet being seen. He lay on his back, pushed his hat over his eyes, blessed the inventor of central heating, and fell asleep.

His dreams were strange and violent and left him, on awakening, with a sensation that he had just lived through something very real. He had dreamt that several people, himself included, were pinned down inside a green wooden boathouse by machine-gun fire from across a river some hundred yards wide. The exasperating thing was that the machine gun was being operated by a child and they were inclined to take foolish risks that the mindless deadly flow of bullets contradicted. Mason, during a lull in the firing, was able to get outside the boathouse and tell those inside where the next bullets would strike. For instance somehow he was able to warn those inside to lower their heads still closer to the floor, (they were already crouching), and to move back from the open door. They had no sooner done this when a storm of bullets punched a succession of holes in the door, splintering the wood. One of the occupants then stood up declaring that he had had enough and was going to make for the open sea. He wore white trousers, blue yachting blazer, pink scarf and spotless white pith helmet. A very pukkah man. No one dared doubt his word.

He dived fully clothed into the water, swam to his yacht, climbed aboard, and disappeared. The yacht had green sails and they were furled and Mason was just asking himself how he would ever get them unfurled without getting shot, when a motor coughed into life, and the water began to churn to the stern of the boat. The yacht drew away. But the machine gun found it, fired across its bows and forced it to reverse, sweeping it into a still backwater like dust before a broom.

Mason saw this diversion as a chance to cross the river and creep round on the child gunner. He swam the river unseen and found himself wandering through lush woodlands, over rustic stiles, making a leisurely way round to surprise the machine-gunner. When he came near the river he heard and saw the child still firing and the people in the boathouse keeping their heads down. When he was about, it seemed, to kill the child, another child came to him and said, 'Do not be hard. Do not kill. He shoots because he has been taught to shoot. Age means nothing. Weapons are ageless. Pity the child.'

He did not kill. Although the dream faded from him then, he remembered seeing a battered scarecrow in one of the fields by the river, and a sense of happiness, of a solution, a move to the green sea. Yet when he awoke in his mind there was the bitter aftertaste of violence.

Scuffling feet and murmuring voices had woken him up. He drew the dust sheet aside cautiously and looked out. His hat got in the way and he took it off. A party was being ushered round, drawn by the elastic bands of community. Mason watched them with one eye. It was funny looking at people from this level, he thought. All legs and big noses. You could see what they were. They all had legs; they moved on them, stood still on them, tip-toed on them, teetered on them; they scratched them, swung them, flexed

29

them. Looking at these legs, trousered and stockinged, move past his hiding place, he found love and amazement in his heart. He began to notice little idiosyncrasies, little habits, that certain pairs of legs clung to. Ones that wanted something more than just to move and stand still.

Then the party left and Mason watched the last pair of legs through the doorway. They had churned dust up from the floor and he had been finding it hard not to sneeze. When he saw the room was empty he gave a great sneeze and wiped his nose on the back of his hand.

Outside in the passageway the last of the party heard, clutched at his companion, and moved quickly forward, a freeze over his face.

Mason dozed a little. Then he took two bananas from his pocket and ate them, wondering what Gonlag was doing with a sackful. He found him difficult to understand. He gave the impression of being forever centred on his own keel, of seeing every storm before it struck and riding it out, head to wind while the storm blew over. Mason found this hard to understand because he was not a sailor and did not admit the validity of the storms and the seas. He had set his course for the Cape Horn of the human soul, whatever that meant, and his course was inflexible, no matter how the wind blew and the waves rolled. It was not in his nature to sail into the wind, and he would reach the Cape, do or die, and see where the oceans of the world dashed and locked horns and where the waves mounted up impossibly high, like Jacob's ladders to heaven, drawing great gulfs of oblivion behind them. And there, he thought, he would recognize at last the awesome forces of which he was but a small expression, and bow his head low.

Last summer, in a way that he could never have imagined, his instinct had set him a course and he had felt himself bound to follow. He was impatient now with the little winds and flurries that upset the trim of his ship. He surmounted them simply by ignoring them, and sailed on, myopic, to the horizon.

It was the quality, (which he had instantly perceived in Gonlag), the quality of being able to ride, surmount and manage to advantage every wind that sent the waves tumbling his way, and with evidence of a kind of loving compassion, that puzzled Mason.

The quality assumed, if he understood it right, a pair of spectacles. And Mason was quite without spectacles of any kind.

The now familiar sound of feet distracted him, and peering out again, his eyes travelled upwards, past sensible feminine shoes, past thick-stockinged legs, past a tweed skirt, past a winter coat and unimposing breasts to the heavy-jowled face of a middle-class female. The woman had stopped before a group and was alternately peering at the full breasts of one of the figures and cupping her hands beneath her own. The silence grew so intense as she did so that Mason hardly breathed. The silence also made perceptions very acute, for quite suddenly she dropped her hands, her mouth fell open and her two eyes swung round and fastened on Mason's one.

He did not flinch. The woman gave a small cry and fled from the room and as her alarm had been great Mason quickly assumed she would communicate it.

He had hardly scrambled out and composed himself thoughtfully in front of one of the stone masterpieces when the woman returned with a man wearing the Museum uniform and a tired and patient face.

'Behind there!' she said, throwing Mason an incredulous glance.

The man stepped forward to his duty.

'Here, madam?'

'Yes, yes, behind there. A man staring up at me! You'll see!' And again she looked hard at Mason.

The man ducked under the scaffolding, lifted the dust sheet and looked behind the statue. He paused and then leant forward, as if picking up something, and drew back, holding Mason's hat between thumb and forefinger.

Mason's hand went involuntarily to his head and his hair crawled. He studied the lines of the group before him even more thoughtfully. The man and woman conferred quickly and approached him, intent.

'Is this yours by any chance, sir?' the man asked him gravely.

'That's right,' said Mason brightly.

'Was it you behind there just now?' he asked even more gravely.

'Who? Me?' said Mason.

The man and woman looked at each other. The woman nodded, her lips tightening.

'Yes, sir, you.'

'That's right,' said Mason.

The man handed Mason his hat which he quickly put back on to his head.

'Thank you, madam,' he said, 'and now would you come along with me, sir?' He ended his sentence on the upward sweep of interrogation but clearly there was no question implied.

'Certainly,' said Mason, 'after you.'

'I thought we might both go together, if it's all the same to you,' he said.

Mason had run into a sudden squall.

The man led him along many passages and past many doors until they entered the vestibule of the ultimate sanctum. Here the man left him (which was foolish), knocked on a door and gingerly disappeared. Mason heard an in-

32

distinct conversation until the door was opened again and he was asked to step inside. He saw a man sitting behind a handsome desk, playing fancy dress in conservative style. When he saw Mason he bent his nose down to a red carnation in his buttonhole and breathed long and deep. Then he leant back in his chair and prepared himself to speak.

'It appears,' he began.

But Mason's nose was as keen as a bloodhound's and he interrupted.

'Pardon me,' he said, 'but your breath really does smell!'

The man in the suit jerked forward across the desk. 'What did you say?' he demanded.

'Something unpleasant, like old mummies, rotten wood and old plaster, I think,' said Mason wrinkling his nose.

The man in the suit opened and closed his mouth, and suddenly turned on the poor man in the uniform who was responsible for the insult. He wanted to know what on earth he was thinking of bringing the dregs of society to him. He had better things to do than expose himself to the insults of the likes, of, of, and he could find no words suitable to describe Mason. The uniformed man began to say something, but he was cut short.

'Please,' said the buttonhole man, 'please use a little discretion in future. I don't want every Tom, Dick and Harry coming into this office.' He glanced at Mason and instinctively sniffed at the carnation.

'He was only doing his duty,' said Mason, 'you ought to give him a medal.'

'Get out!!' said the buttonhole man very strongly. He lifted some papers from his desk and put them down again.

'Come on,' said the uniformed man glumly.

He led Mason through the Museum to the revolving door at the main entrance.

'That's what you get for putting on a uniform,' said Mason.

'Piss off!' said the uniformed man.

Mason swung the door round and round until it was revolving at speed and then he engaged himself in it and whirled through and out into the cold.

The sky and the air was of some dull grey substance, a counterfeit, a travesty of the element for which lungs are created. Nevertheless all about him people made their ways, busily peering into shops and faces and shops again, searching on someone else's behalf for their heart's desire. A sign in a shop window winked on and off, wishing him a Happy Xmas, which he rejected.

It was already dark. The museum was forgotten. He was ready for the night. As he walked along the pavement a well-known carol deafened him. It came from a loud-speaker hung over the door of a surgical appliance shop. He at once crossed the road and was nearly run-down by a double-decker bus. The carol hummed out above the traffic and for a long time it was in his ears.

He plunged into the backstreets and wandered steadily and with a deliberate tread until the day was gone and half the night too.

Then he thought it time to make his way to Marble Arch.

4

Gonlag was fast asleep, yet even sitting there on the parapet with his head nodding, there was something that set him off, something discernible about him. Mason smiled as he walked slowly along the pavement towards him. It was the first time he had smiled that day. He hated Christmas.

When Mason sat down Gonlag woke up.

'Hello,' he said, after he had seen who it was.

'Hello,' said Mason. 'How are things?' It wasn't that he particularly wanted to know, it was just that he wondered if he would say it again, as it seemed, Mason had found out, he always did.

'Never seen things brighter,' declared Gonlag and in spite of his sleep. Mason smiled again in the night. 'How was the Museum?'

'All right until I was thrown out,' said Mason.

Gonlag laughed and asked how it had come about. When Mason finished he laughed again. 'You're a lucky sod,' he said, summing it up.

Everything was as it should be. The policeman, the taxis, the hot-dog stalls, the women, and the men, all in their places, come from all corners of the city to rendezvous until the morning. The traffic from the West End dwindled as if someone had blown a whistle and turned a stop-cock and only a few cars could leak through. It was only just turned midnight but then, it was England.

A cold wind blew across Hyde Park from the Battersea Power Station, bringing subtle odours. Mason sniffed the air disgustedly, and then he sniffed again, incredulously.

'Don't think I'm being personal,' he said, 'but do I smell perfume?'

'You *are* being personal and your nose deceives you. You smell bath soap. Special bath soap.'

Mason digested this astonishing fact in silence.

'The fruit and vegetables?' he asked presently.

Gonlag nodded. But he wanted to change the subject. 'I knew a chap once,' he said, 'he used to come here at night, same as you and me, and he used to get into the Reading Room of the British Museum. He said he'd written off to somebody, the bloody Prime Minister for all I know, to ask for permission to read the books on astrology there, and they'd let him in. He said he used to wash his socks down in the washroom and dry them under his seat all day. Spent most of his time sleeping I think. He spent most of his time here chewing my ear off and telling me I had a great future. And when I laughed he said he didn't judge a life in pounds sterling and nor did God. So I put that in my pipe and smoked it for a while and I rattled the coppers I had in my pocket and felt happy for a week at least.'

Mason said nothing.

'You want to write in and tell them you want to study the Vagrancy Laws,' said Gonlag; 'you'd be all right then.'

Mason still said nothing and Gonlag put the back of his hand to his mouth and cuffed away a yawn.

The night was settling down. There was to be no frost after all and luminous clouds moved across the sky. Mason leant back against the railings and watched them go by. He loved their extremes; how you could look at them on a summer day and hear them moving on feather dusters and then, when the weather was right, out of those silences would come nothing less than thunder.

'How did you go selling the vegetables?' he asked.

'Not bad,' said Gonlag. 'Five and six.'

'I got half a crown,' said Mason, 'walking up Oxford Street. A man carrying parcels collided with me and I helped to pick them up, so he patted me on the shoulder and gave me half a crown. Do I look *that* down, Gonlag?'

'Well,' said Gonlag, 'you'd better not ask me, we're two of a kind. It's always hard at first, on the road.'

Neither of them talked for a while. Gonlag watched the women by the taxis, making little expressive movements with his hands. His hands were deep in his pockets, which marred their expressiveness, but kept them warm. He gave out a big sigh and looked at Mason and Mason looked at him and they had to laugh.

'One day,' said Gonlag, 'I'm going up to one of those whores and I'm going to say "I've got no money, but I'm bursting, so how about it! Just how about it!"'

They laughed quietly again.

'No,' said Gonlag, 'I sold the stuff to a woman. Lives off Church Street. She asked me to make it a regular order, and that means a regular income and that's just what I wanted this time of year. How about that for a good bit of luck?'

Gonlag slapped Mason on the back for good measure and as Mason had been leaning forward and studying his boots he nearly fell off the parapet. He coughed.

'Steady on!' he said. 'It's the woman, not the money. You can't fool me.'

Presently Gonlag said, 'Would you like a hot dog? I've got the money.'

'No, thanks,' said Mason, 'since today I'm a vege-

37

tarian. But I've got half a crown, would you like a
woman?'

They laughed again.

'Good to hear you laugh,' said Gonlag, 'bet it's blowing
the cobwebs away.'

Mason muttered something inaudible.

A voice growled then, from along the parapet. 'Can't you
keep up a civilized conversation,' it went, 'without beseech-
ing Heaven to smite you in twain for your filthy laughter
and profanities!'

'Sorry, Vicar!' said Gonlag. 'I didn't realize we were in
church.'

'And so you are!' the growl strengthened. 'In God's
Church!'

'Amen,' said Mason solemnly.

A policeman appeared, bringing silence and watchfulness
with him.

Pity the Creator of man, thought Mason, who only
asks us to be joyful. Who gave us mouths and hearts to
rejoice with and who hears instead nothing but tales of
worry, fear, despair; who gave us eyes to delight with and
has instead to see our visions in chains. Imagine a crowded
street and one man there in the thick of it leaning against
a lamp post in a sky blue suit and a rainbow tie whistling
the tunes of God and the motor car, and all around him a
grey sea of worry and despair. Perhaps that is the man. The
Scarecrow Man in a sky blue suit.

'God bless you, constable!' said Mason, as the policeman
towered past them. The policeman paused and considered,
shooting both Mason and Gonlag an impersonal glance,
and walked on.

When he was out of earshot Gonlag asked Mason if he
hadn't taken leave of his senses.

'No, no! I'm coming to them, I'm coming to them!'

cried Mason, suddenly feeling himself trembling and excited. 'Look! I must tell you about the Scarecrow Man, Gonlag, I'll tell you tonight!'

'Take it easy,' said Gonlag, worried at this outburst. 'Take it easy. And who is this Scarecrow Man?'

Mason unleashed a flood of talk, so confused and seemingly irrational that Gonlag held up his hand, even more worried.

'Listen,' he said, 'start at the beginning. It's a good place to start.' He was ever ready to hear something new to mill on the stones of his mind, but it had best be understandable. He sensed he was about to hear the heart of this man and he didn't want any misunderstandings or ambiguities.

There was a pause in which Gonlag, despite himself, startled Mason by putting a hand to his chest and jumping suddenly to his feet. 'Sorry,' he said, 'I don't want to put you off your story but you had me forgetting again. You haven't any papers with you, have you?'

Mason shook his head.

'Right then, here you are. I've got enough for both of us again.' He pulled out a bundle of papers and gave half to Mason. Mason stood up and they stuffed them under shirt and trousers. They were a little less than chill from the warmth of Gonlag's body.

When they sat down again Mason said nothing. He was waiting to be prompted.

'Sorry about that,' said Gonlag. 'Go on then. Let's hear it from the beginning.'

Mason thanked him for the papers and told him.

One of the most vivid memories of his youth was of the scarecrow. He remembered the headmistress's legs. They were mottled blue and red from being too near too many fires. They bulged. He remembered firing rockets from the railway lines at oncoming trains. He remembered lying on

39

the outskirts of a gypsy camp watching petrified because he believed everything he was told and fascinated because he was still young. He remembered shitting in his trousers. He remembered picking red poppies and fighting, and many other things. But of them all the scarecrow led the procession of memories and when all the rest drew back and faded one by one, the scarecrow stayed behind, gaunt and alone.

The scarecrow never seemed to change. It was always there in the middle of the field, ragged, hatted, arms outstretched to all the storms and the rains and the sweet winds. Only once did he climb over the fence and look. The head was a worm-eaten swede and the arms and body and solitary leg were sticks with stuffing bound around, and then old clothing on the top. After that he never went near to look again. He looked from a distance and saw as he wished to see. He saw the body and the legs and the beaten old face and the wide-open arms and the hat pulled down and a seagull or a blackbird perched on top, pecking or looking about.

That was childhood and youth. The time came when the reaper reaped the corn, the golden stalks shuddered and fell flat upon the earth and revealed, with one stroke of the scythe, the distant fields and hedges and hills where before all that could be seen was as far as a field-mouse could run and a tossing fringed corn-stalk sky.

Mason paused and straightened his back. Gonlag, who knew a long story when he met one, settled back against the railings and pulled his hat far down over his eyes, as Mason continued.

Last summer he had worked down on the south coast. He'd met a woman, a waitress in a seafront café, and he'd lived with her. It was a small town, the café customers were regular and it had not been long before the locals knew about it. There was no one who seemed to mind. She had a child, a five year old girl. She had been good to Mason and he'd been sorry in a way he hadn't loved her. He had got a job as a kitchen porter and learnt more about that business than he could ever have imagined.

Gonlag interrupted.

'I knew a bloke who was a kitchen porter once. He got the sack and the manager wouldn't give him his money, he was such a mean bastard, and they often are. So he waited until they were busy again in the evening and walked straight through the front door and up to the manager and told him he if he didn't give him the money he'd tell everyone he had the syph'. Anyway the manager told him to clear off, so the bloke backed away, put a hand on his balls and started shouting out that he'd no right to keep his money just because he'd got the pox, and what would the customers think, eating their lovely food. Well, a crowd started gathering and in the end the manager went up to him and put some money in his hand and off he went.'

'That took some doing,' said Mason.

'Desperation,' said Gonlag. 'He didn't fancy starving.'

Mason's story began to run within him now like an underground stream. His words were springs which welled to the surface and ran on a little way and submerged again. He had hardly noticed when Gonlag interrupted. His story flowed on. It reminded him of the dream, it had the same flow and rhythm. He was aware of the silence when Gonlag stopped talking and eventually said, 'Anyway,' pulling his coat around him and settling his head well down into his collar, so that all that could be seen was an ear and a hat perched on top, 'Anyway, go on.'

He leant back and half-closed his eyes so that everything became more blurred than usual. The street lights mingled with the traffic lights and the traffic lights blurred with the greys of the road and pavements and the hot dog stalls, the

41

taxis, the men and the women all blended together with the filtering colours, congealed fluently and lost their definities and shimmered, so that everything swam outside the waters of his half-obscured vision as it would if they were taken to the bottom of the sea.

Without moving he asked Gonlag if he had a cigarette. Gonlag put half a one in his outstretched hand. When it became apparent that neither of them had a light, he gave it back again, thanking him.

The story was within him again, running and flowing.

'Have you ever had a moment,' he said, 'when it seems that a certain wind blows and you look, and everything, all the leaves, grasses and flowers, everything, is pointing the same way? Do you know what I mean? As though you had been given a sign?'

Gonlag made no answer, sunk within his coat.

'Anyway, that's how it was for me last summer on the south coast. It wasn't the last big wind, if you follow me, but it was strong enough, strong enough to sail by. If you're ready for it, as I was, it was all that mattered. I had a dream you see.'

Mason looked up at the sky. A smoky orange night filled his eyes, as if he lived in the middle of a ball of cold candy floss.

'I dreamt first of all of a mountain stream. I followed it along until it began descending in a series of waterfalls through a wooded glen, full of larch and mountain ash, to the sea about a mile away. It was a hot sunny day and it had been raining, making the stream swollen and the falls thunderous.

'The next thing I was bathing under the first, the topmost waterfall. The water splashed over me so hard I had to hang on to the root of a tree. It was a giant mountain ash and it grew right at the edge of the fall. I can see the roots of the tree now. That water had washed some of them clean and they were yellow-green and fleshy-looking, like snakes. There was one that hung down suspended, as though it had been grown there specially. It had a knot of black fibrous roots at the bottom which made it look like a lion's tail. It was this that I clung to against the force of the water. I clung to it and pushed myself out into the waterfall and the water splashed down on to my chest and fell away from my thighs. I never felt anything so good, so life-giving, as that water. I became part of it. It was as if the water was the river of life and I was splashing around in it.

'I can remember that happening normally, the water was fast and it splashed and gurgled and thundered, just as you would expect it to, and then suddenly everything went into slow motion. The root of the tree I was hanging on to broke, the lion's tail broke, and very slowly the water pushed me back and down and the last thing I saw, normally as it were, was a leaf lying in one of the dry channels that the water must only have reached when the stream was very full. It was cupped, beached, waiting for the rains. Then I hit my head against a smooth rounded black rock in the water and the fall itself seemed to reach out and fill my face and lungs, until I drowned.'

Mason began to get excited again, it was so clear in his mind. He could see the falls in the orange sky, an orange stream and black basking rocks, a giant tree growing way above the sky and just those twisted shining roots curling down out of heaven.

Gonlag stirred, bent forward and spat on to the pavement. Without looking at Mason he thrust his head back inside his coat collar. Mason knew he was listening because he had left his ear exposed, and that was a sacrifice on a cold winter night.

'Well,' said Mason, 'that was in slow motion and everything that happened after that was in slow motion too. I found myself, not at all to my surprise, standing up in the water again, wading through it under the waterfall and through the rock over which the water fell, until I was there among the rock and the earth and the drumming of the water and the tree roots and the darkness. But it wasn't really dark because there were small lights, like precious jewels, glowing there, like sapphires or burnt umber, and I wandered in this way among the things of that world until I saw the Scarecrow Man coming towards me. At first I thought it was just one of the jewels glowing more strongly than the others, but the light grew and grew until there he was, the Scarecrow Man.

'He took me by the hand and said, "Come, let me take you where you want to be." And he led me out through the earth and the rock and the waterfall. We went through the water and over the falls and played in the fine rainbow spray a moment, then we went down through the trees until we came to the sea. We skimmed the waves like seabirds and travelled on and on. I never knew such happiness.'

Mason was silent a moment and Gonlag popped his head up out of his coat collar and said, 'Are you all there or aren't you?'

'No,' said Mason, 'I'm a spook.'

'I knew you were different,' said Gonlag. 'Is that the lot?'

'That was just the dream,' said Mason, 'there's more to come.'

'I was afraid of that,' said Gonlag, 'and I need my beauty sleep too.' He receded again under his coat collar and Mason heard a muffled, 'Carry on.'

'That was the dream anyway,' said Mason, 'and that was what made the leaves all stand in the same way, that was the certain wind I'd been waiting for all my life, the one that made sense out of nonsense, that made five out of two times two.'

'Some wind,' came Gonlag's muffled voice. 'I wish it had been blowing on my side when I was at school. I needed some support.'

The dream was gone. Mason sat forward on the parapet and put his hands on his knees.

'It's good for me to tell you this,' he said, 'if you don't mind listening. It makes it all come clear to me. The next morning, after the dream that is, I woke up and found on my tongue, "The Scarecrow Man." Just that. I turned over and told my woman. I felt I had to tell it. I shook her until she was awake and then I said to her, I was very excited. I said, "The Scarecrow Man", two or three times. All she did was give a little shriek, pull the bedclothes over her head and tell me to go and take some liver salts.

'After that things changed. The funny thing was I didn't remember the rest of the dream until the middle of the day. I saw a photo of a waterfall in an advertisement for cigarettes or lavatory paper or something and it all came back. I couldn't tell anyone then, certainly not Betty, this woman. I changed my job and went on the buildings, concrete gang, because I could see the break coming, and I knew I'd need the money.'

Gonlag nodded. His hat waved solemnly to and fro three times above his coat collar. He said nothing.

'All I wanted after that was to find the Scarecrow Man again! I began asking people if they knew him, if they'd ever seen him, ever heard of him. I began to ask them as if it was a joke but they soon knew I was serious, Betty saw to that. I even asked the other blokes in the concrete gang. I asked so many people that the children began to shout after me, "Scarecrow Man! Scarecrow Man!" But I didn't

45

mind. Why should I? All I wanted was to find him again, or simply know who he was. That was the first step, the first thing I had to do.

'Then one day, we'd been pouring concrete all day in the rain, you know, it was one of those pours when you start and then the rain comes and what can you do? You can't stop. So that was it, and not for the first time on that site or any other I suppose. We were wet through and tired and one of the gang, Harry (had a face like a butcher's fist), said to me, "You don't have to look any further, mate. You look more like a scarecrow than anything I've ever seen in the fields!" I walked over to him and hit him hard and short in his silly stomach and we started scrapping. We both got the sack, though they started Harry again later, so I heard. It was a silly business. Normally I'd have laughed, because it was funny. But just that once it was too much.'

'I know how that is,' said Gonlag. 'I don't blame you.'

'Yes,' said Mason. 'I was ashamed of course and wanted to shake hands but Harry turned his back and walked away. In the end, Betty, my woman, got so worried she took me to church the next Sunday.'

'What!' said Gonlag. 'Not marriage!'

'No, no. She'd heard all about it and thought if she took me to church it might get me sorted out.'

'Clutching at straws,' said Gonlag. 'That's dangerous though, letting a woman take you along to church.' He laughed.

'Well, she was desperate. There was so much gossip,' said Mason.

He would have continued with his story but sounds of a scuffle to their right made them both look sharply in that direction. They were just in time to see one man bring his knee up into another's groin, and at the same time crack his head down into the other's face. The man at the receiv-

46

ing end crumpled down against the railings and slid on to the pavement and the other walked quickly away.

'Trust the Law,' said Gonlag, 'to be out of sight.' They got up and walked towards the man who was sitting motionless on the pavement.

No one else made a move. The taxi men, the hot-dog men, the women and the homeless over along the parapet, all seemed to have seen and heard nothing. So little was that familiar night scene disturbed that Gonlag and Mason felt a slight eeriness overcome them as they walked towards the man. They began to doubt the evidence of their senses. It was as though a boulder had been thrown into a lake and the water had opened and closed and made no splash or ripple.

When they came to the man they found it real enough. 'Poor bastard,' said Gonlag, 'that's the first time I ever saw a man use his head and his knee at the same time.' They helped the man to his feet and sat him on the parapet. Then they moved him back to where they had been sitting. The stone was warmed there at least. The man was very sore and sorry for himself. He held one hand to his head and one hand to his balls. The first thing he said was, 'Where's my hat?' It was not on his head. Mason went back for it and found it on the pavement. It was a bowler hat and he brushed it with his sleeve as he walked back which didn't make it any cleaner. The man thanked him when Mason put it back on his head.

Gonlag was saying, 'What did you want to let a man do that to you for? You're old enough to vote aren't you, and you didn't even mark him.' The man was in fact middle-aged and patently professional. For the moment he was quite crushed. 'Let him alone,' said Mason, 'he's still in pain.'

'Missed the last train, dammit,' the man muttered

47

between his teeth. 'I knew something like this would happen.' He hadn't really seen either Mason or Gonlag yet because he was too taken up with the pain. They were still nothing but voices.

Presently his pain eased. He took his hand from his head but left the other one where it was and made an effort to pull himself together. All this time, even when he had been hit, the man had made no cry of pain, not even a moan. Mason reached out and turned his face towards a street-lamp and examined it. His nose was unbroken, untouched it seemed, but a smooth round swelling stood out on his forehead. 'He's lucky,' said Mason.

'You're in luck, matey,' said Gonlag to the man, 'if you can see it that way. He could have flattened your nose for you.'

The man nodded his head and lifted a hand to his bowler hat to correct the trim. 'It felt as though my whole head had been smashed for a while,' he said.

'It would do, it would,' said Gonlag. 'You rest easy for a while. Would you like us to call a copper?'

'Oh, no, thank you very much,' said the man, smiling brokenly at the pavement. In the muddy yellow street-lighting his face looked very ill. He was still in pain. He pressed both his hands to his groin and held them there.

They watched him recover.

He was well dressed and most probably worked in the city. Even in pain he articulated, with the few words he had spoken, in that peculiar way adopted by those who deem their breeding entitles them to lead, (and who cosily assume that there are also those who want to be led) and wish to make it immediately apparent.

When he seemed better and had straightened up a bit, Gonlag asked him the question that had been bothering him.

48

'Why didn't you mark him at least?' he said. 'You could have slipped him one surely!'

'I simply couldn't,' said the man. 'That's all there is to it.' He looked about him then for the first time and saw Mason and Gonlag. All at once he looked like a bird ready for flight.

Gonlag couldn't let him go without finding out why he had been hit, and taken by surprise as well. Mason had lost interest and was staring blindly away into the depths of the Edgware Road.

'If you must know,' said the man, 'I was thinking about other things when this fellow came up to me, and I didn't know he was violent until he had proved it pretty conclusively.'

Gonlag persisted. 'Oh dear,' he said blankly. 'Why not?'

The man looked more than ever ready for flight but clearly felt he was under some kind of obligation, so he said, 'This fellow came up to me, so close that I couldn't see his face. It was in shadow. And he asked me straight out if I were a queer. I said I wasn't and he said I was. I said I wasn't and he said I was again. It was very childish. And then he hit me all of a sudden.' He spoke in a flat cool voice and when he had finished he pulled the cuffs of his overcoat down and cleared his throat.

Gonlag burst into laughter.

This was too much for the man and he was making moves to get up and leave them when he caught sight of the women by the taxis, and it was as if he had remembered something, for he pulled himself back and settled again on the parapet, still looking at the women.

He turned to Gonlag and Mason. 'A cold night,' he said, trying on a smile. They readily agreed it was. 'I suppose you're quite used to it though,' he said, 'you fellows, eh?'

'Never get used to it,' said Gonlag. 'Just as you're getting

49

adjusted to winter, along comes spring and upsets the apple-cart.'

The man laughed at this but very absently. They knew the signs, because they had sat there on that wall before and watched the women and felt their stomachs sometimes jump. They knew the signs from inside out.

'We'll keep a look out for that merchant,' said Gonlag, more to the night than to anyone else, 'if he comes round here again.'

'You and who?' said Mason, and coughed lightly. Gonlag looked at him and shrugged.

The man was quite absorbed in himself but he managed to say, 'You men, you mean you stay out here every night, in this weather?'

'Certainly,' said Gonlag, 'and why not?'

'Well,' said the man, 'it seems to me, er, a little hard.'

'Never,' said Gonlag. 'We get the air off the park, pure oxygen, and bags of exercise. We don't over-stuff ourselves because we can't; we take women when we can, which isn't often; and best of all, we, or I anyway (I don't know about Mason), I never get worked up about justice and injustice, truth and untruth, because you've got to have money and stuff for that kind of luxury. And we know better than to get beaten up by a maniac.'

The man digested this and then he said, 'Chacun à son goût,' all the while absently and staring hard towards the women.

'Why don't you go and be done with it, then,' said Gonlag.

The man started, and began to contradict and thought better of it. He felt inside his coat for his wallet and said, 'I don't do this sort of thing often, you know.'

'Of course not,' said Gonlag, enjoying himself. 'You don't look the type.'

50

The man braced himself as if on the threshold of something momentous and stood up uncertainly. He smoothed down his coat and flicked his right arm in a special way, producing a thin band of white shirt cuff.

'Lovely white shirt,' said Gonlag. 'Pity about the bump. How's your balls?'

The man was embarrassed. He towered above them now, the rounded proportion of his hat definite against the lurid sky, and the long black coat sweeping down towards them. Gonlag and Mason looked up and studied what they could see of his face.

He was bringing himself to say something.

'Look,' he said, 'it was very decent of you two to help me out. I might have been badly hurt, and Lord knows I could have been.' They watched his hand go under his coat and bring out a wallet. He pulled out a pound note. 'I'd like you to have this,' he said, 'and buy yourselves whatever you like.'

He gave it to Gonlag.

They both looked up at him in silence, with blank faces.

The man looked towards the taxis and said with an attempt at joviality, 'Right, I think I'll be on my way now. A very happy Christmas to you both and thank you again. Yes. Good morning.'

They watched him walk towards the taxis and noted the animation, only slight, that his approach caused. He tipped his hat to one of the women and after that they lost interest and looked away. It had happened before.

'Quick recovery!' said Mason.

Gonlag spat on the pavement, hard. 'How about that then, Surzo?' he said. But the question was plainly rhetorical and no answer came.

They heard the taxi draw away, but they didn't bother to look up.

51

'I don't know,' said Gonlag forgetting all about the man, 'things are good for me this Christmas somehow.' He thought about the woman and was silent.

'The pound's yours,' said Mason. 'You did the talking.'

'Never,' said Gonlag. 'We'll split it down the middle. The poor bastard, though. Typical middle-classed specimen. You could see it all over him, from the knot on his shoe-laces to the snot on his nose. It wasn't his clothes. It was the air about him. Condemned to masturbation, school-books, and matrimony, and when they've found out what it's all about, if they ever do, it's too late.' Gonlag spoke with compassion but he spat on the pavement all the same.

The night was not so cold now. Heavier clouds moved across the sky, dully reflecting the city's glow. It would rain.

Gonlag settled himself into his coat, after looking at the sky and tugging at the brim of his hat. 'Go on,' he said, 'you were saying? Your story?'

Mason had been saying the story all the time. It had only gone underground. 'Where was I, Gonlag?' he asked.

'Your woman was taking you off to church, to get you sorted out,' said Gonlag.

He had been listening.

Oh, yes, thought Mason. This was the part when the wind blew stronger and the leaves fairly flew from the trees. The scent was strong. All I had to do was to go forward, to follow. Or so I thought. But it was not so simple as that. Nor was I really ready to move, as soon as I found out. All clocks were not yet turned to the beginning of the world.

Mason told the rest of the story, so far as it went.

'There's not much to tell really,' he said, 'not in so many words. The actual facts don't add up to much, but their implications changed the whole course of my life. Well, as I said, Betty took me along to church. I'm like that child

52

who said "Samson!" when she was asked who her favourite character in the Bible was, "Because he pulled the temple down." Have you ever smelt a parson's breath? I have. I had breakfast with one once. He was a Jesuit, but what does that matter. He talked all the time, his face was grey, and I just couldn't believe my nose. Comes from hearing too many confessions and being torn by envy at the sinner's freedom and frustration at not being able to forgive himself. Of course he was proficient, I expect, and well able to say the words required of him. He smelt of anti-life.

'Anyway, there we were, sitting in the church, just like the song. We knelt down, Betty pulled me down (no stopping a determined woman), and we stood up. Then we sat down and then we knelt again and then we stood up and sang a hymn and watched the Vicar being escorted to the pulpit by a verger carrying a fairy wand to turn the Vicar's tongue to gold and silver. The verger and the Vicar bowed to each other and the Vicar went on alone into the pulpit like Moses into the mountain, put his hands together and donated his sermon to the glory of God. Then he began to talk to us about the Church Roof Appeal Fund.

'Betty was on the edge of her chair. She put her hand in mine and gave it a happy squeeze. She really thought we were on to something. If I'd had half her enthusiasm then, I'd be wearing my collar back to front now if I'd got one.

'I watched the man closely. I saw his dog collar left a red mark on his neck, and that although he was young, no more than you or I, he had high blood pressure.'

'Too much good living,' said Gonlag. 'Few weeks with a pick and shovel would have put him right.'

'He was going slightly bald, just at that spot where the hat rubs the crown. I could see it because he was forever pushing himself back from the edge of the pulpit and coming in low again, as if he was doing the butterfly stroke. I can't tell you much more about him except the most important thing. His eyes were wet, and there wasn't a featherweight of joy in the man's whole body. He was all wind. He'd got it all worked out, cut and dried.

'When I'd seen enough of the Vicar I started looking around the church. I'd been too busy genuflecting (there's a word for you, Gonlag!) and standing and sitting to have a look around before. Betty wasn't any better than me. She kept an eye on her neighbour and a hand on me. I was looking around, as I said, when I saw this figure. It was the Scarecrow Man. But not so you would recognize him. I had to stop myself getting up and putting my hat on his head and my coat round his shoulders. I suppose you'd call him Jesus Christ, but I knew better. There were other figures like this one in the church, but none of them was the Scarecrow Man. Only that one. It didn't look like him, mind, not like my dream, but when I saw this figure, it all came together. The scarecrow I saw when I was a boy, the Scarecrow Man in my dream, and then this figure, they all connected up and it was like a current passed through them to me. It sort of lit them up, and they held hands and smiled at me and I got so excited I nearly jumped up out of my seat. I had my glasses on so I knew there was no mistake. I looked and I looked and this figure seemed to flood with light and the scarecrow in the field began to dance and the Man I had seen in my dream smiled and smiled.

'Betty started making little noises, I was squeezing her hand so hard, and then it was too much, the Vicar was still sounding off, and suddenly I could see it all so clearly, so clearly, and I jumped to my feet.'

Gonlag was sitting forward, hands on knees, watching Mason.

'I stood up,' said Mason, 'and asked the Vicar who the

54

Scarecrow Man was. I said. "Do you know who the Scarecrow Man is?" '

'What happened?' asked Gonlag. 'What did he say?'

'I can't very well remember,' said Mason, 'because Betty still had hold of my hand and she was trying to pull me down, and people all around were telling me to shut-up, but all very subdued, and then Betty started crying, and the Vicar said very sweetly that if I had anything to discuss with him perhaps I'd see him afterwards in the vestry.

'Well, I saw he didn't know and couldn't know, and it was all so clear to me still. So I gave Betty a pat on the back, walked along the row, and left the church.'

'Didn't anyone stop you?' asked Gonlag.

'No,' said Mason. 'Nobody tried.'

5

In the morning they went, as was becoming their habit, to Covent Garden. It was Christmas Eve. When Gonlag said, 'Two to Covent Garden,' and pushed the pound note under the till, the man raised his eyebrows but otherwise looked as unconcerned as ever. They shared the change between them.

As it was Christmas time the supplies of all fruit and vegetables were intensified at the markets and the two men quickly filled both their pockets and the sack, which Gonlag had carried inside his coat. But he wasn't satisfied.

'There's just something else I'm after,' he said, and made his way to the flower stalls. He spoke to one of the men there and Mason saw the man give him two carnations, a crumpled rose and another flower, the name of which he didn't know. Gonlag came away all smiles but he would say no word of explanation to Mason. It wasn't really necessary though.

The sack wasn't large and was easily carried. Gonlag humped it over his shoulder gently, put the flowers carefully inside his coat pocket, with the heads sticking out and winked slowly at Mason.

They presented quite a spectacle when they opened the café door and went inside. Mason had a general impression of a swivelling of cloth caps in their direction, and reflected that if he wore glasses still they would have misted over in the warmth and the impression would still have been equally blurred.

When the teas and the bread and butter came they set upon it seriously, eating and drinking with great reverence, more than it deserved. Feeling carefree, with the day clear before him Gonlag sucked and smacked at the hot sticky tea with an abandon that drew comment from several of the other people in the café, 'Give him a straw, Doris!' gaining the ascendancy.

But Gonlag was unperturbed as ever, smacked his lips with gusto, put the cup down on the saucer with a clatter, smiled all round and got up out of his seat. He marched to the counter and asked Doris for a refill, two refills. He brought two fresh cups back to the table, smiling all over his face because he had remembered the efforts he'd made trying to drink the woman's coffee silently. He shook his head.

Mason had been all the while sitting at the table, thinking about the next day, Christmas Day, Christmas Day, Yuletide, Xmas. Xmas made it sound like algebra. It was very fitting. Let $X =$ whatever you like. A cipher for an unknown and unrecognized event. Now if $X =$ the Scarecrow Man! He knew it did! He only hoped to see the end of the next day this side of the prison bars. But he would do it.

Gonlag put the cups on the table noisily, to announce himself, and Mason looked up. Then he saw for the first time that they were not alone at the table. An old man shared it with them. He had come in when Gonlag was up for the teas. The old man took a square parcel from his coat and unwrapped it. Presently a small tape-recorder lay on the table in the folds of the brown paper. Gonlag and Mason forgot their tea.

'Good morning, gentlemen,' said the old man.

'Morning, guv'ner,' said Gonlag. Mason nodded his head and smiled.

The old man fetched himself a cup of tea and when he came back he pressed a button on the machine and the wheels whirled.

'I expect you've been collecting fruit and vegetables as I have,' he said.

'That's right,' said Gonlag. 'Good pickings today.'

'Yes,' said the man, 'good pickings,' and sipped his tea, pressing another button and freezing the flapping wheels. He could see they were interested in the machine, so he said, 'it's for the wife. She can't get out of bed. Last three years. So we got this and I sometimes take it out with me and play it and let her hear, well, just the sounds of everything, so she can hear how things are, sort of.'

Gonlag and Mason were so fascinated they said nothing.

'I brought it out this morning so she could hear Christmas Eve,' and he pressed another button still and the wheels began to slowly turn. All three men stared at the machine. The cafe door opened and shut, feet sounded on the boards of the cafe, somebody belched, everybody talked, so that it really did seem like a buzzing. Doris said, 'Two cups, dear? Right?' and tea cups and saucers continually rattled together.

The old man quickly, on impulse, stopped the machine. He looked at the other two men. 'Would you,' he said, 'mind saying a few words to my wife? Just wish her a Happy Christmas, that would do. I'd be very obliged to you two gentlemen.'

Gonlag shifted in his seat and Mason covered his mouth with the tea cup.

'What,' said Gonlag, 'speak into the machine?'

'It's very simple,' said the old man. He pulled out a small microphone that had been tucked in his belt and pressed the button to make the wheels move slowly. He pushed the microphone to Gonlag and whispered, 'Her name's Millie.'

Gonlag swallowed.

'Um,' he said. 'Well. Hello, Millie. My name's Gonlag.'

'That's fine, that's fine,' said the old man.

'And,' said Gonlag, 'I wish you a very happy Christmas.'

'Oh, thank you,' said the old man. He pushed the microphone then at Mason's chest.

Mason put down his cup and stared at the old man.

'Say a word to my wife,' said the old man softly, nodding his head. Mason was as unprepared as Gonlag.

'You're not missing much here,' he said finally. 'But I wish you a very, a very happy Xmas.'

The old man nearly clapped his hands together, but instead he pressed the button to stop the machine. He smiled. He had two front teeth.

'You've got more than me,' said Gonlag, 'look!' He grimaced to show his gums. He felt foolish but he wanted to do something.

'Ha! Ha!' said the old man. 'I'm seventy-four you know. And the missus is seventy-one. I never had a day's illness in my life. And we've got a parrot at home that drinks tea just like you.'

Mason and Gonlag laughed.

'Go on!' said Gonlag.

'Yes,' said the old man, wagging his two front teeth. 'She likes a brass band best of all, with lots of pigeons.'

He drank up his tea and wrapped up the machine.

'I'll get some more on it,' he said, as he got up out of his chair, 'before I go home. Then she'll have plenty to listen to when the Queen's speaking. Well, mustn't hang about. Been nice meeting you gentlemen. Happy Christmas!'

'Same to you!' said Mason and Gonlag together.

They watched him go.

It had begun to rain. Little translucent pebbles rolled down the misted windows and bumped gently at the bottom. The men who came in now steamed a little, little wisps climbing up from their wet clothes, and a secure cavelike feeling stole over the cafe. Doris behind the counter, commander of the tea urns and all she surveyed, felt the change come over her cafe and was pleased. She became a refuge, more female, softer, as these steaming men came in out of the drizzling dark of the early day and asked for tea. But she gave nothing away. Her tongue maintained its hard dominance. Only her heart warmed within her.

They had drunk their tea and it was time to go. Gonlag carefully humped the sack and they made their way out to the nearest Underground station to have breakfast. It wasn't raining hard, but it wasn't the weather for an open-air breakfast.

Down under the streets they found a bench on the platform out of the way of the morning rush, when it came. They ate a breakfast of bananas and oranges and when they were licking their fingers, Gonlag said,

'I was wondering if you'd do me a little favour, Mason?'

'Tell me what it is,' said Mason. He was tired and wanted nothing more than to sleep.

'All right. I can trust you,' said Gonlag, 'I know that. It was when you were telling me about your Scarecrow Man.'

'Not mine,' said Mason.

'Well, it was then, anyway,' said Gonlag, 'when you were talking away last night that I knew you were the one to give me a hand.'

'Go on,' said Mason, 'tell me.'

'Right!' said Gonlag. 'The woman I sell the stuff to lives in a place that's got the decorators in. That means paint and that's just what I want. And a brush if there's one handy. I only need to borrow it for the night, and I'll return it next day. I need you to be a decoy, or see if the coast is clear, you know, just to help.'

'O.K.,' said Mason, 'but I won't take any risks because I don't want to be inside on Christmas Day.'

''Course not,' said Gonlag, 'but why?'

'Because the reason I came to London was to go to church on Christmas Day and say whatever I think I have to say.'

A train thundered in, the doors rolled back and three people got out. It thundered away again, sucking hot air after it.

'You're a funny bloke,' said Gonlag. 'You'll get nicked for that, that's something certain. You just can't bust into a church and take over, if that's what you aim to be doing!'

'I'm not going to "just bust in". When the time comes I'm going to climb up into the pulpit or whatever there is and say whatever is inside me. And then I'll climb down and walk out, like I did before.'

'Blimey!' said Gonlag.

'Only this time,' said Mason, his face lighting up in the gloom. 'This time I'll have something to say!'

This was Christmas all right, this was, thought Gonlag, grinding his gums and staring at an advertisement on the other side of the lines. He stared hard and as he stared he began to see the growth of a plan. If Mason would help him, well then, he could help Mason. But it would need some thinking about.

Finally Gonlag said, 'That'll take some doing. I hope you'll get away with it. But look, all I want you to do is just come along with me when I go to see this woman today. Then we'll see what it looks like.'

'What do you want the paint for?' asked Mason.

'Oh,' said Gonlag, 'that's hard to explain. Don't think I can—it's just that one night, not long after I'd gone on the road, I came across this bloke called Surzo, and he told me things, this and that, and well, it's a bit like you really, I want to paint them on walls, so that everybody can read them.'

'Surzo,' said Mason. 'That's a strange name.'

'He's a strange person,' said Gonlag, and determined to say no more.

'O.K.,' said Mason. 'I'll come along, if it's only to see your woman!'

Gonlag laughed.

'I told her we'd see her at two this afternoon, so I'm going to sleep till then,' he said.

They went to sleep. They had bought tickets for Notting Hill Gate and these they held in their hands, forgetting all about the rainy world above them, and hearing only the successive rushes of the underground trains that seethed through their sleep like an unnatural tide.

They were disturbed by a Negro station porter who was trying to sweep under their bench. His great white grin spread itself out of the gloom and he said, 'S'cuse me, gennelmen,' and giggled.

Gonlag and Mason lifted their feet. The platform clock told one o'clock. 'You're better than an alarm clock,' said Gonlag. 'Timing couldn't be better.'

The Negro grinned again.

'Fellers like you back home,' he said, 'but they sleep on the beach.' He rested his cheek on his hands which held the top of the broom, and looked at them.

'Not when it's raining,' said Gonlag, 'I'll bet.'

'Just climb back under the palm trees, man,' said the Negro, 'and go on sleeping there.'

'What a life!' said Gonlag.

'You're right,' said the Negro. His eyes rolled up and away down the dingy platform. The whites of his eyes were streaked with red. He said, 'Anyways, it ain't respectable,' took his cheek from his hands, pushed the broom around the platform again and moved gradually away from them on a zig-zag course. 'S'long,' he said.

'They don't know what they're chasing,' said Gonlag quietly.

The next train that came in, they caught. It was the rush hour, or one of them, and Gonlag was anxious for his flowers and fruits and vegetables, Mason was anxious for nothing, and the people standing around were anxious not to get too close to either of them. They emerged from the Underground like corks from a bottle.

It was still drizzling slightly from a whitish oppressive sky and the wind blew cold off the shiny pavements. The hand Gonlag held the sack with turned white and then red against the cold. Mason had both hands deep in his pockets, down among the apples and the bananas. As they closed in upon the street Gonlag began to feel a tingle of excitement he hadn't felt for so long it was almost a joke. Not knowing whether it was the paint or the woman made him irritable.

The decorator's van was there, neatly parked, backing against the rain. The firm's name was written on the back and sides in red lettering. 'H. G. Mullen & Sons Ltd. Painters and Decorators,' it read. The men were nowhere to be seen.

Gonlag said in a near whisper, 'There it is, that's the van and that's the woman's place.' He hesitated. 'I'll introduce you to her if you like, but I'd like it if you go as soon as you can because she's, well, she's nervous. You know, she's nervous.'

It was unlike Gonlag to repeat himself.

63

'Don't worry,' said Mason. 'I'll hardly step over the threshold. I'll just pop in and out.'

Gonlag looked relieved.

They were abreast of the van. On the pavement were two metal extension ladders. But no paint and no brushes. A corner of the curtains in the woman's window twitched. He swore.

'We've been spotted,' he said. 'It's no use now. I was hoping to go up the stairs and see where they were working and where they left the paint. If I don't go in now she'll wonder where I've gone. Have to wait another day.'

He stood under a blackened cherry tree, considering. The rain fell silently. Mason was peering in the back of the van. 'There's no paint in there,' he said. 'Tell you what! You see the woman as you would anyway and I'll go on upstairs to spy out the land. Then I'll come back, put my head round the door and clear off. You never know. There might be twenty tins of paint up there with my name on.'

Gonlag's eyes lit up.

'Thanks,' he said. 'Take it easy, though.'

'Don't worry,' said Mason, 'I'll do what I can. What colour do you want?'

'Eh?' said Gonlag. 'Well, you could . . .' and then he grinned.

They walked up the steps, through the front door, and went inside.

'See you later, then,' said Gonlag, winking heavily as he knocked at the door.

Mason did not answer but bounded up the carpeted stairs like a greyhound, turned the bend, and was out of sight. Then he turned and leant out over the banisters and was in time to see Gonlag drop the sack to the floor, and smooth his hair back under his hat. Then the woman opened

64

the door. He couldn't see her. 'Hello, where's your friend?' he heard her say. Gonlag's reply was indistinct, and then the door was shut and he was alone.

The banisters were of wood, dark and dusty, and the stair carpet, which had once possessed a pattern of roses, was now threadbare. He walked on up the stairs passing door after door, each numbered and painted with a dark brown Victorian kind of varnish, the nemesis of colour. The house had the damp silence, the cold respectability, of the tomb. It felt as though it had been built on an old graveyard and it was not hard to imagine gravestones leaning against the cellar walls and white mushrooms spreading their canopies in the dark.

But Mason's nose was phenomenal. He prided himself on it. His eyes were auxiliaries, to be used as a dog might use them, to finish off the work of the nose. He could smell this house now so keenly that it almost amounted to an extra-sense, beyond the range of smell. He had smelt the woman's perfume when she opened the door to Gonlag. He had known its absence when the door was shut and it sank like sand thrown on water and the silence came again.

Mason's nose told him now that the decorating men were at work, not far ahead, a few storeys perhaps, and indeed he could hear them. He smelt cigarette smoke and paint drawn across the damp gloom, and it made him think, of all things, of beach umbrellas and the heavens opening and raining frogs and fishes.

He walked on up the stairs, pulled himself up round a bend and suddenly came face to face with himself. Opposite him on the landing was a huge mirror. It occupied half of the entire wall, and he watched himself advancing, step by step, full length, towards himself. When his nose at last touched the cold glass and his eyes swam before it he breathed slowly out. His warm breath spread out in a mist, so that he could no longer see himself. The mist spread out quickly, almost splashing, it seemed, and then drew back like a tide, until all was as before and Mason confronted himself in the mirror, sharp and clear against the gloom, again. He wondered how many people had done the same thing.

Then he breathed out hard two or three times and the warm misty tide raced out over the cold glass and hovered there. Mason stared at the mist in front of his eyes and was aware of the impetus lost and the reaction imminent but not yet active, and of the hairbreadth moment when all the possibilities in the world might be fulfilled; and then the tide turned implacably and crept back upon itself and foundered somewhere near his nostrils, where a slight trickle of life escaped.

Mason held his breath and all the mist disappeared. Several beads of moisture gathered on the glass and started an erratic downward journey. He was a child all at once, a child with a puzzle. He held his breath till his lungs were bursting and let it go with a rush. Then he said the simplest thing he could think of. 'The sun rose yesterday, the sun rose today, and the sun will rise tomorrow.'

He stood back from the mirror and clapped his hands for joy. The joy affirmed itself, hard and durable, within him and he felt as he had sometimes felt as a child. He did a childish thing. He bit his finger so that the blood came and smeared it in a curve over the glass. Then he turned away and walked on up the stairs.

The smell of paint was now so strong that it overpowered the pervasive smell of the house. Mason heard whistling and the slip-slapping of paint brushes echoing tinnily in an empty room. He heard one of the men say, 'Easy with that brush, son, we only want it on the walls,' and the unperturbed whistling of the other and the steady slap-slap which was only broken for him to say unexpectedly and with the utmost concision, 'Carpets.'

Mason crept forward now, up and round the last creaking bend in the stairs. When he gained the landing he saw unbelievably stacked outside the door of the room that was being decorated no less than six tins of white emulsion paint. I'll risk this, he thought to himself, I'll risk this. He had only to creep forward, put one of the tins inside his coat and creep off again. The whistling and the slapping of the brushes continued as blithely as ever. A fart sounded. The older man said, 'Pardon,' and the younger man said, 'At your age,' and this so reassured Mason that he went forward and took the paint. He put the tin inside his coat (it made him look pregnant), and was away. But as he turned, a lavatory chain was pulled and a cistern clankily emptied and a dark unnumbered door farther down the passage was unlocked and opened. Mason jumped with the fright and without taking thought hunched himself over the paint in a very clumsy disguise. When a man finally came forth from the lavatory, senile and silver-bearded, Mason was hobbling towards him, possessed by the most atrocious limp, touching his hat and saying in a deep west country accent, 'Good afternoon to 'ee, Squire!' The man was astonished enough to reply in kind with a 'Good afternoon to you, my good fellow!' But he spoke too loudly for Mason's ear and as soon as he had rounded the stairs he left his hobbling behind and raced down, past the mirror on which he turned his back, to the first door on the right past the door.

He drew breath and knocked. The quick surety of female footsteps and the door was opened, flooding him with the sweet perfume he had now smelt twice before. It was too sweet really. He hardly needed to use his eyes. A womanly

67

woman full of that animal certainty that sometimes makes men in comparison seem like aimless mayflies. Her breath was awful. He wondered if that deterred Gonlag.

'The fruit will do you good,' he said. 'You want to eat all you can.'

The woman was taken aback. She spoke over her shoulder to Gonlag, who was not to be seen. 'Is this your friend?' she asked him.

'That's him,' came Gonlag's reply.

'Oh, well,' she said, 'come on in, won't you?'

'Thank you,' said Mason.

Gonlag appeared. His eyebrows were raised in mute questioning, until he saw the bulge in Mason's coat, and then he clearly couldn't believe his eyes. The woman was looking at the bulge too.

Gonlag cleared his throat. 'Sylvia, this is a mate of mine. Mason, this is Sylvia, touch hands and come out fighting.' They shook hands.

'He gave me some flowers,' she said to Mason, 'I'll go and put them in water,' and she hurried to the kitchen.

'Is it?' said Gonlag incredulously.

Mason drew the tin of paint dramatically from his coat and swung it by the handle. 'It is,' he said.

Gonlag was lost for words. He took it in his hands and muttered something about Surzo. Then he said, 'We'll make it tonight then!'

'We?' said Mason.

'Yes,' said Gonlag. 'You and me!'

Sylvia came back into the room from the kitchen then, carrying the flowers in a small pot.

'What have you got there?' she asked.

She looked from the tin to Mason's flattened coat and said, 'Jack of all trades, isn't he,' giggling and nudging Gonlag possessively.

68

Gonlag grinned foolishly and moved to put the tin near the door, where his sack also stood.

'What lovely flowers!' said Mason maliciously as Sylvia put them on the table.

'Aren't they,' she said. 'He just gave them to me. Would you like a cup of coffee, um, Mason, wasn't it? I'm just making one for us both, and another won't make any difference.'

Mason sat in the chair and Gonlag and the woman sat on the bed. Mason was enjoying himself.

'Miserable weather we're having,' he said.

'Isn't it awful,' said Sylvia. 'But then what do you expect this time of year?'

'True, true,' said Mason, 'but if it's going to be seasonable I wish it would snow.'

Gonlag snatched up his coffee and sucked at it mightily through his gums. They all laughed.

'There you are!' said Gonlag.

Mason sat solidly there until his coffee had gone and he had declined the offer of a second cup, to Gonlag's visible relief.

When he was leaving Sylvia said, 'Why don't you bring him along tonight, Gonlag.' Then she turned to Mason before he could answer, and said, 'You like films, don't you?'

'She's an usherette,' said Gonlag.

'What's the cinema?' asked Mason.

'Excelsior, the local one,' said Sylvia. 'I start at five so you come in any time after that. I'll be there and so will Gonlag, won't you Gonlag?'

'I won't be anywhere else,' he said.

It was agreed, and Mason let himself out of the front door and into the street. It was still raining. At least it was more like a heavy mid-afternoon dew than anything else.

69

It polished the roads and pavements, made the black cherry trees glisten and after a while hung in small coloured half-moons from the brim of his hat. He stopped by the decorator's van and then walked backwards a few steps to look at the house. Supposing they were all like that, he thought, all the houses in this street. He saw again the dark airless landing with the great mirror at the end and his blood smeared across it. He imagined an old Irish caretaker woman dusting around with an old pair of bloomers, not noticing herself in the mirror, just seeing the dried blood smear and scratching it away with her fingernails and moving on again, following her duster like a waterdiviner a hazel stick.

Mason was suddenly overcome with a feeling he couldn't define. He whisked his hat from his head and whirled it high into the air. When it came down it caught in the branches of one of the cherry trees and he had to shake it down, covering himself with drops of water from the tree.

It tumbled out of the branches into the gutter and he put it back on his head, satisfied, and walked lightly away down the street.

6

Mason took an apple from his pocket, washed it in a large puddle, dried it on his coat and took a good bite. He passed a cake shop safely, and then a modern clothes shop, for young women principally it seemed, in and out of which young things stepped jauntily and bravely. He pressed his nose to the window fascinated. When one of the two shop doors was opened, pop music rushed out upon the street and a solemn bus queue, slightly embarrassing them, not belonging. The queue shifted its balance like a restive cow at milking. Across the road a military garrison defended itself against civilians behind high glass-topped walls, and at either side of the recklessly open gate stood two soldiers, on guard. The idea of anybody actually wanting to break in there seemed very remote and the alternative presented itself that those inside were always trying to break out. This idea was strengthened in Mason's mind when he saw a tight little group of white-kneed runners in green-and-white striped vests come dashing out through the gate before the very eyes of the sentries. The sentries moved not a muscle and the runners and their twinkling knees soon lost themselves up the street in the Christmas crowds leaving the garrison behind them where knives were sharpened and boots were polished. It was a drab cancer in the street.

He walked on down the street and when he passed

beneath a galloping Father Christmas, he crouched, slightly, apprehensive. The reindeer were galloping, that is, and Father Christmas rode behind them in a chariot, cracking a whip in a magnificent commercial frenzy.

He was within the orbit of a famous store. A well-bred choir sang to him the story of Good King Wenceslas and seduced him, he couldn't help himself, into the air-conditioned warmth. He found his way erratically to Father Christmas himself, jostling as he was jostled, watching the faces of the people.

Father Christmas was holding court in the Father Christmas Grotto to a steady flow of big-eyed, open-mouthed subjects. In one corner of the Grotto a smart-looking man in a grey suit with a plastic name-tab in the lapel watched to see that the Christmas spirit didn't exceed the limits of commercial common sense. Father Christmas had as much to say to the mothers as to the children. Father Christmas had a funny white beard and bloodshot eyes. Father Christmas was half-sober and when he spoke it was like opening the door of the boozer on a Saturday night. He was the second Father Christmas that week. The man in the grey suit had sparrow eyes.

The choir, broadcast, burst into another carol, 'Ding Dong Merrily', the people in the store moved about like a shoal of feeding fishes, and Mason, believing he was witness to a kind of madness, turned into a pike with a long cruel fish's snout and sheared through the crowds and out into the cold airy street.

With his feet on the pavement again he didn't stop until all the sounds of Christmas were far behind him. He shook them from his ears, those jingle-jangle, ding-dong sounds, and breathed in the dying murky light of the day. The street lamps clicked on. It had stopped raining but the roads were still wet and cars and buses and even an occasional bicycle made nervous sounds as they zipped along. As the cars and buses passed, Mason caught glimpses of hats and faces and shopping bags and parcels where someone had smeared a sleeve over a misted window. It was nearing the rush hour so he decided to walk to the Albert Hall and make his way to the cinema through the park.

When he reached the Albert Hall he saw on one of the notices that Handel's *Messiah* was being performed there that evening, Christmas Eve, at seven-thirty. He walked round the walls of the hall and thought about it. 'Yes,' he said to himself, 'that's what! And the walls! Gonlag can paint whatever he likes on them, they're big enough. If he wants to paint anything, this is the place.' So he decided, and cut away into the Park.

All at once he found he loved his life. He discovered it, just like that. He wandered and he saw, he heard and he discovered. If he passed a baby in a pram he would some-times stop and watch its hands opening and closing like sea-anemones and its dumb glistening mouth mouthing wisdom unheard of in the Houses of Parliament, and he would say the first words that he found to the tiny dumb ears and go on his wandering way. And now tonight he would stand in the cold outside the Albert Hall and hear the coming of the ever-present Heaven on earth, with both ears open, and a heart as light as a robin.

He knew then that he had been right in coming to London, and he would accept anything that might happen in the morning. His heart was glad.

In the Park the lights were on and as he walked and the night descended the people he passed looked furtively at him and away again in the shadow of an atavistic fear. The lights cast yellow puddles of light on the pavements and the earth and in and out of these Mason paddled, squinting against the glare. Soon he had crossed the Park and heard the flow of traffic again on the other side and seen the lights of the Bayswater Road.

The cinema was open and ready for business. It was ten past five. He bought the cheapest ticket and pushed through the swing doors into the dark again. A voice whispered. He showed his ticket. 'No need to have bought one,' the voice chided. It was Sylvia. She guided him with the torch into the back row, where he trod heavily on somebody's foot and was surprised to hear Gonlag's voice raised to curse him. Sylvia flicked off the torch and turned away. When Mason had sat down he leant towards Gonlag and said, 'Does she carry that torch for you?'

Gonlag was not amused and told him to shut up and watch the film though Gonlag himself wasn't watching it at all. He was watching Sylvia flick her torch up and down the aisle and walk with that sure high-heeled femininity. She was good, thought Mason, who was also not watching the film, she was good at standing in the aisle half-way down, flashing the torch impatiently down a row of seats as a luckless patron stumbled to a resting place, and slightly turning her hips so that she presented a silhouette far more arresting than anything on the screen. For Sylvia was attainable. As Gonlag continually proved when she came back to stand by his seat and he ran his hand up under her skirt.

Mason pulled his hat down over his eyes and tried to concentrate on the film. For once he wished he had glasses. It was in its death throes anyway and the lights soon went up. Sylvia had vanished and Gonlag was sitting back with a pleased and cynical expression on his face.

'No point in wasting time at our advanced age, is there?' he said, leering slightly in spite of himself.

'Good to see she thinks the same way,' said Mason.

A succession of advertisements, from the most abject

74

fauning to the frankly belligerent, followed each other across the screen. A man climbed across Gonlag and Mason and sat down in the next seat.

'I'm sorry,' said Gonlag. 'That seat's taken.'

'Who by?' he said. 'The Invisible Man?' But he moved along all the same.

'Move along,' said Gonlag to Mason. 'Sylvia.'

When they had settled down again, Gonlag said, 'How on earth did you do it? How did you get the paint so easily?'

'It was out there waiting for me,' said Mason. 'All I had to do was pick it up.'

'That's Surzo for you,' said Gonlag. 'I knew it was right, all along.'

Mason thought about the *Messiah* and the Albert Hall and said, 'Gonlag, I've found a good wall for you and something to listen to while you're doing it.'

Gonlag pricked up his ears, leant towards Mason and whispered, 'Where?'

'The Royal Albert Hall,' said Mason. 'They're having the *Messiah* there tonight.'

'What,' said Gonlag, 'in person?' He wanted time to think about the idea. 'The Albert Hall, eh?' he muttered to himself. Sylvia walked past but he didn't notice her. She was piqued.

'What time?' he asked.

'I thought about ten o'clock. It starts at seven-thirty,' said Mason.

'Well,' said Gonlag, 'you certainly thought of something there. I'll have to get Surzo's O.K. but if it goes all right, I'll be indebted to you, Mason. You didn't get a couple of brushes did you, while you were up there?'

'A couple!' said Mason. 'I thought you could use news-papers.'

'And I thought you were going to help me,' said Gonlag.

Mason sighed. He had to be free on Christmas Day, to solve the equation, to declare the X.

'I might,' he said, 'if it looks safe.'

'Don't you worry,' said Gonlag, 'it'll go like a dream. Surzo'll see to that.'

The lights dimmed, music sounded, the curtains drew back and the film stabbed the darkness and spread in dimensions across the screen. The cinema! The camera followed the flight, in Technicolor, of a spear. The audience watched it arc through the air and bury itself, like a mustard seed, in sandy ground. There it stayed. It had been the herald of war. Following it across the plain on a more direct route came a body of sternly-galloping Roman cavalry.

Mason settled back in his seat, pulled his hat still further over his eyes and gave himself up to sleep. He would have liked to have watched the film, but sleep claimed him first.

Gonlag nudged him in the ribs.

'Sylvia wants to know if you'll come to a party tomorrow.'

Mason nodded his head. Booze, he thought. If I'm still my own master. The iron-hooves of war thundered over him and he went to sleep. He was aware of Sylvia sitting down next to Gonlag, and of her occasional giggles and of suggestive underhand rustlings, but he wasn't interested enough. He sat tight as a coiled spring, waiting, he thought, the touch, the time, the moment.

7

At a few minutes past ten Mason saw a figure hurrying along the street towards him. He squinted hard and saw first of all the tin of paint, which the figure was carrying by the handle, then the walk with a roll to it and a merry bend in the spare elbow, and then, when the figure was almost upon him he called out, 'Hello, how are you?' It was a silly-sounding thing to say out there in the damp cold round the Albert Hall, but it was for the sake of the answer that he said it.

'Never seen things brighter,' came the reply. And there was no doubt about it. It was Gonlag. By the look of things he'd never spoken a truer word.

'Came on quick as I could,' he said. 'Got held up.'

'I know,' said Mason, sniffing. 'Had your oats did you?'

Gonlag swung the tin of paint in his hand and said, 'Here, I brought it, but we're going to have to use our fingers for the painting. Paper's no good really.'

Music sounded. From within the Hall there came a fortissimo union of full choir and orchestra that burst through the closed doors and windows, the roof and the solid masonry itself, like the concussion from a heavy bomb. Gonlag was busy trying to prise the lid from the tin of paint. A car drove past them and then a straggle of people and they moved further back around the Hall.

Mason was summoning all his powers for the great moment in the music. 'Won't be long now,' he said.

'What won't?' asked Gonlag, still unable to open the lid.
'The bit,' said Mason.

Gonlag grunted, gave the penny he had put under the lid a great bang with his left boot, which he had taken off, and the lid pumped into the air and rolled a little way down the pavement on its side, leaving a thin white spoor like a snail. Gonlag retrieved it and put it loosely back on the tin.

'How long have we got?' he asked.

'Perhaps ten minutes,' said Mason, 'then they'll be streaming out.' He had his ear to the music, listening, and only half-heard what Gonlag told him.

'All right then,' said Gonlag, 'this is what I want you to write. Are you listening?

SURZO WON'T TAKE MUCH MORE!
BEWARE!'

'Have you got it?'

'Just that?' asked Mason.

'There's more after,' said Gonlag, looking around for a good wall. The Albert Hall was no good because it was too irregular and ornate. In the end they chose the Royal College of Art, which had smooth black walls, ideal for the work they had in hand.

They hurried across, looked quickly around to see if anyone was watching, and set to work. The single pot of paint forced them to work together.

'Really big now!' said Gonlag.

While Mason hurriedly wrote his piece and strained his ears for the music, Gonlag wrote in big dripping letters:

SURZO IS READY TO BUST OUT! BEWARE!

They used first one finger, then two or three, and finally the whole hand, pushing the cuffs of their overcoats back away from the paint. The paint spattered on to the pavement and freckled their boots and trouser legs. They worked more and more feverishly as the music began what must be the final chorus. Gonlag kept furtively peering to either side, but no one passed them, not even the shape of a policeman's helmet loomed in the night.

Gonlag stood back from their work, full of excitement and admiration. He saw a good crack in a paving stone and said, 'How about that, Surzo!' It was as if he were addressing a prisoner in a fatal dungeon. Mason looked in astonishment at Gonlag and though he heard no reply from below the pavements he saw Gonlag's face light up with pleasure.

'Right,' said Gonlag briskly from between his gums, clapping his hands together and at once regretting it, 'now the next lot. I don't know, Mason. We're not messing about you know, Royal Albert Hall, Royal College of Art. When this is done I'll make you a Knight of the Garter!'

The music began a steady and long crescendo.

'We've not long!' said Mason anxiously.

'Don't worry about it,' said Gonlag. 'Don't worry about a thing!' He was waving his white-painted hands about, doing a little dance in front of the great white announcements on the wall. He almost kicked the paint over and then at once came back to business. 'This time,' he said, as they confronted the black walls of the College, 'this time write:

SURZO IS THE FIRE WITHIN THE EARTH
AND HE WARMS MY FEET AT NIGHT.'

'Anything you say,' said Mason, dipping his hand in the paint and mouthing the words. But he was listening to the music, waiting for the moment.

They worked quickly. Gonlag worked with extreme gusto,

79

paint everywhere, and Mason worked quietly and rather absently.

Mason was writing WARMS when he heard the moment approaching.

'What's the matter?' asked Gonlag.

Mason held a finger to his lips. Then he crossed the road and pushed one of the side doors of the Hall open. The music poured out into the street, and he stood there in the full flood of it. Gonlag had finished his sentence for him and came across to stand with him, looking back at their work, absorbed.

Mason listened. The music shook free of the apocalypse, and the women, glorious in their voices and finding the door of Heaven in their hands, took the full force of the combined orchestra and choir into themselves and flung the door open, so that all the world that had ears to hear knew beyond any doubt that Heaven and Earth were become, and were always, one.

'Amen,' croaked Mason and sat down on the pavement, crying.

The music had ended. There was adequate applause.

Gonlag coughed and scuffed his feet.

'They'll be down soon won't they?' he said. 'Let's clear off!'

So they crossed the road away from the Albert Hall and watched from behind the railings of the Park, hiding their hands. Already people were coming from the Hall in increasing numbers, and cars revved up and doors slammed.

'Shhh!' said Gonlag, for no reason at all. 'Someone's looking. A lot of people are looking!' He was excited. Mason had to take his word for what was going on. Things were blurred.

A group of people stood round the messages from Surzo

80

and even at that distance Gonlag could hear the laughter. He cursed and spat hard.

'Come on,' he said, 'they're laughing! I didn't mean it for a joke.' He still held the tin of paint, which was far from being emptied, and they decided to leave it inside the door of Sylvia's place, in case, said Gonlag, they might need it again. As they walked their hands shone significantly white. Somewhere they would have to wash them.

'Are you sleeping with her tonight?' asked Mason.

'No,' said Gonlag, 'I don't want to see too much of her. It's all right the way it is. Beats me why she goes for me anyway. I mean, look at me!'

They laughed happily, and then walked on in silence, in and out of the shadows, just as Mason had done earlier that evening, alone.

Mason thought about the music he had just heard. Why was it that applause seemed so futile, so puny and so necessary? Supposing at the end of the music just now, when the conductor had dropped his baton, the orchestra had relaxed and eased their instruments, and the choir had sung their last note, supposing then, in the silence, no one had clapped, no one had stirred, and the echoes had faded one by one? What would have happened? Then the seats and the carpets and the light bulbs and the stones in the walls and the beer in the bottles of the snack bar would have sung their praises loud, and the great Hall itself would have danced. But instead of that the people had put one hand upon the other and clapped, and made the sign for all things and themselves, in witness of the event.

'Actually,' said Gonlag, 'I've got a bottle of wine. I got it to celebrate what we've just done. They can laugh their heads off, so long as I don't have to watch them I don't mind. I reckon we done well.' He could almost hear Surzo rumbling beneath their feet, saying something like, 'You

81

bums done a good job. I wanna congratulate you,' and so, he thought, who cares if they laugh. Yes, he even liked it, the laughing.

'I don't mind if they laugh,' said Gonlag again. 'In fact, I like it.'

'Good,' said Mason, 'that's the style!'

'Well, what do you say about the wine then,' said Gonlag. 'Do you fancy a drop or don't you?'

'Nothing I'd like better,' said Mason, for it was a cold night.

'Don't get carried away now,' said Gonlag. The bottle bumped cosily against his leg as he walked along, a solid comfort.

Mason stopped and rubbed his white hand in a small pile of old leaves, and Gonlag did the same. They were nearing Sylvia's street. The paint still stuck to their hands and so when it had dried they put them in their pockets, out of sight.

'A couple of marked men,' said Mason.

Gonlag laughed.

'But we certainly put it on that wall though,' he said, 'we certainly did it in fine style!' Then he spoke in the accent Surzo spoke with. He said to Mason, 'I sure am indebted to you, buster, I sure am, sure I am.' He was also light-headed.

'Forget it,' said Mason. 'I had a good time.'

'I won't forget it,' said Gonlag. 'You wait and see. You wait.'

The plan was forming in his mind.

But Mason, of course, didn't know what he meant.

'It was a pleasure,' he said, 'and we didn't get nicked.'

8

Gonlag sat down and bounded up again as if he had sat on a trampoline instead of the grey cold parapet. Mason, who was already sitting down, blinked. The illusion of Gonlag's not having sat down at all was strong.

'What's wrong?' asked Mason.

Gonlag stared away up the Edgware Road, shrugged, and sat down again.

'Nothing,' he said. 'It's just the first time I ever forgot to get any papers.'

'It doesn't matter,' said Mason, 'we'll just get cold.'

'That's right,' said Gonlag. He looked up at the night sky. 'I can see it on that big black wall now. Great white letters! Beware! Surzo speaks! Ha!' He brought his hand from his pocket and looked at it, grinning away to himself. They had washed their hands in the lake finally, but it hadn't made much difference. He put his hand back in his pocket.

'I'm now going to ask you a silly question,' he said. 'Have you got a bottle-opener?'

Mason had not.

'Ask a policeman,' he said. 'Your friend and mine.'

The stage was set the same as always. Hot-dog stalls, taxis, men and women, yellow street lights, dark green shadows. From the West End traffic flowed steadily. It was not yet midnight, the stop-cock was not turned. Cars stopped by the hot-dog stalls and business was brisk. The women too were busier than usual. There was a rumour of festivity in the air. The cars remained cars, yet they gave off something different, as if passing under all the coloured lights and Christmas trees and suspended electric stars had given them a crackling aura with which they glowed as they careered away into the numb limbo of the suburbs. The people inside these cars were silhouetted cardboard figures, motionless and unreal. It was the machine that whirled around the Marble Arch and away like a comet, scattering stardust and tinsel from the Milky Way of Oxford Street at Christmas time.

It seemed that way to Mason. He looked at the traffic and at the traffic lights and noted the damming and flowing of the traffic. Then, as naturally as the rain falls, he saw the Scarecrow Man. The one who strode across the fields and ditches, into the dark declivities of small woods and out again, pacing easily beside the clakkety train with long, stilting strides, arms ever outstretched, flapping and tattered, spreading joy, embracing everything, blessing the train he accompanied, with the birds swooping and calling around him; the Scarecrow Man who Mason had looked at all through the journey to London, nose pressed to the window, journeying with him to the city, now appeared again. Mason watched him step out into the flow of traffic from the far side of the road, seeming to part the traffic like the river Jordan, and cross the road towards him. He closed his eyes because he didn't need to see any more.

When the train had begun to lay through the outer London suburbs like an iron sword and the houses and the streets and rivers had fallen away to either side, at that moment the Scarecrow Man had halted before an advertisement for cigarettes fifty feet long and twenty feet high, birds had flown away from his shoulders and he himself had disappeared. The rivers were so dirty they looked like

84

flowing excrement, the houses and factories looked worn, charred, and sick, and everywhere chimney-pots, battalions of chimney-pots rank upon endless rank of them, looked poised and at last ready to march off and storm the citadel and hold all humans hostage. Only the advertisements were full of colour and light, making a mock of what they fed upon. Against this background the Scarecrow Man faded and disappeared.

Since that time Mason had not seen him, though he had looked for him ceaselessly. His search hadn't been adventurous. It was inward and passive, and he had known he would see him, perhaps when he left London again after Christmas. But now here he was walking across the road towards him. The Scarecrow Man.

He heard the traffic flowing again. Gonlag stirred beside him. He heard footsteps coming nearer and nearer.

When Gonlag spoke he didn't at first understand the words.

'Evening, officer,' he said. 'Have you a bottle-opener anywhere about your person, perchance?'

The policeman had held up his hand and crossed the road on a pedestrian crossing. It was very simple. Mason opened his eyes and saw the policeman regarding them from above his chin-strap. The policeman became the policeman. Mason was unabashed. He had seen the Scarecrow Man coming towards him across the road and he was as sure of that as he was that a policeman now stood before them.

The policeman rummaged around in his mind, though not in his pockets, for a reply, and presently said, giving his words the same sort of weight his black polished boots gave to the pavement, 'A bottle-opener?'

'Well, a corkscrew will do as well,' said Gonlag carelessly.

'I've seen you two here before, haven't I?' the policeman said.

'That's right,' said Gonlag.

The policeman teetered thoughtfully, looking away and over their heads into the dark depths of the Park. Then he looked down at them again, his dark eyes inspecting each of them in turn. His eyes were hedgehogs.

'The police have better things to do than to supply a couple of layabouts with corkscrews in the middle of the night,' he said conversationally. 'I think you'd better be moving along now.'

He stepped back to give them room to move along.

'Certainly,' said Gonlag.

'Glad to,' said Mason.

The policeman glanced quickly around the scene, saw the taxi-drivers were looking his way and said in a voice that gave no room for any argument, as if there was any, 'Come along, move along there now!'

He spoke so loudly that one of the forms along the parapet jumped, scrabbled himself together, and shambled away, muttering. Mason and Gonlag had hardly had time to get stiff, but when they rose to their feet they made a great show of easing tired and aching limbs. The policeman grew impatient with them, put his hands behind his back and walked slowly away, humming an indistinguishable tune to himself and no one else. It could have been a carol.

'Layabouts, are we!' said Gonlag, grinning at Mason. 'Fucking law!'

'He didn't look more than twenty-five,' said Mason. 'You've got to laugh.'

'Anyway,' said Gonlag, 'he did us a favour. It was getting cold and we would have moved sometime or other anyway.'

The policeman had wandered off around the taxis and

they stopped their stretching and walked off in the direction of Notting Hill Gate, for the very good reason of finding something to open Gonlag's bottle of wine with. A corkscrew would do.

'We'll find something,' said Gonlag.

They walked up the Bayswater Road and left Marble Arch at their heels. Part of the audience had left, but the show went on.

They found the Portobello Road and turned down it. It was darker there, shadier almost. A place where life might have undertones that the garish open streets precluded, and the song of the city changed key, almost dropped an octave. The pubs were long since shut and the two men had the empty street to themselves. The bottle of wine banged against Gonlag's leg as he walked and that and their footsteps were the only sounds to be heard above the deep cumulative hum as the giant city sprawled around them in its early sleep. The chances of opening the bottle seemed very slim.

'Looks as though we'll have to crack it open and spit out the glass,' said Gonlag.

Before Mason could have replied a voice from a cobbled side alley, conscious of the night and the stillness and the irrelevance of the human voice and accordingly hushed, said, 'Psst! Excuse me! Do you think you could give us a hand?'

Two young men came out of the cobbled alley and showed themselves under a street lamp.

'Help with what?' asked Gonlag.

The two young men looked at each other.

'Well, we've got a piano here,' said the shorter of the two. He spoke with an Australian accent. 'And there's a party down the road and we want to get it there. It's too much for us and we wondered if you'd give us a hand.'

'Where is it? I can't see it?' said Gonlag.

'It's in there,' said the shorter one. 'Back in the alley a ways.'

Mason and Gonlag looked at each other and then into the alley, but they couldn't penetrate the darkness.

'Show it to us,' said Mason.

He and Gonlag followed them into the alley. Gonlag pulled the bottle from his pocket and held it by the neck. Mason moved his weight to his toes and walked lightly as a cat.

From the darkness there came the sound of a hand smacking down on to the top of a piano and the unmistakable twanging echo followed, and when their eyes had become accustomed to the comparative darkness the shadowy form of an old upright piano did indeed become discernible.

'This is it!' the short one said.

Gonlag put the bottle back into his pocket and Mason shifted his weight back to his heels again.

'Right,' said Gonlag, spitting on his hands, 'where to?'

'Down the road a way,' said the taller one. 'It's very good of you to help.'

As they walked to the back of the piano, Gonlag said to Mason, 'We'll be all right for a corkscrew now.'

The piano had four tiny wheels and when the four of them put their shoulders behind it, it moved with squeaks and bumps stubbornly over the cobbles. It made such a noise that an upstairs light shot on across the road and despite the cold a window was pushed up and a head darted out.

'What the hell do you think you're doing this time of night?' said an authoritarian voice.

'What's it look like,' said the shorter one.

With an effort they pushed the piano out on to the crown

of the road and pointed it downhill towards the traffic lights. The noise the piano made drowned the voice of the man in the window. It had become a live thing. Its strings quivered and sang in a strange discordance that was somehow akin to the damp-smelling night. It stood at the top of the hill, planted its four small wheels in the crest of the road and twanged and creaked with excitement.

'Bloody beatniks!' shouted the man at the window, though he was only a little way away from them, on the second floor of an antique shop.

The shorter of the two original piano-movers spoke then in a tone calculated to freeze the bossiest person. In a voice straight from the land of the free he said, 'Go back to bye-byes, ya drongo.'

That was the signal.

The four men put their shoulders low on the piano and moved it slowly out, over, and down the hill. The man at the window shouted more abuse. It must have left his lips like thunder for above the rumbling, twanging, shivering, progress of the piano it sounded like the squeaking of a bat. The men bent their shoulders, Gonlag clutched the bottle in his pocket, Mason held on to his hat, and the piano moved faster and faster down the hill.

Mason began to laugh hysterically. 'Happy Christmas!' he bellowed. Gonlag began to laugh too. They were pushing from behind, watching the black road stream beneath them and jagged red sparks fly out from under the wheels, and they laughed and they laughed, and their laughter too was drowned in the great rumbling noise from the piano and they laughed even louder and pushed the harder. They sweated and the piano lumbered down the hill.

'Stop!' shouted the two in front. 'Stop pushing! Traffic lights!'

But Gonlag and Mason had no intention of stopping, and

laughing like maniacs they pushed all the harder. The piano
shot over the road junction in a sharp flurry of sparks, hit
a ridge in the tarmac, jumped into the air, and drew to
a swaying halt on the other side of the road. Two hysterical
and breathless men clung to its hollow wooden sides, and
chortled like children. The traffic lights blinked noisily in
the silence and turned green, and the two young piano-
movers crossed the road and came up to the piano. They
had prudently stopped before the red of the traffic lights.

'You fellows all right?' they asked.

Mason waited. Gonlag rarely missed an opening.

'Never seen things brighter,' he said.

'Just couldn't seem to hold the piano back,' said Mason.

'Yes,' said Gonlag, 'going too fast. That was the trouble.'

They rested then around the piano, leaning on it, and
breathing hard into the clammy night. It was so quiet all
of a sudden no one wanted much to be the first to speak.
But Gonlag was only waiting to get his breath back.

'Do you do this often?' he said.

They laughed quietly and good-naturedly, showing teeth
and shrugging shoulders. The taller of the two walked round
the piano, inspecting.

'Lost a wheel, back right,' he said.

'What did you expect?' said the other.

'I expected them *all* off!' he said. He lifted the lid with
an impatient gesture and played a few abrupt chords and
then ran a thumb up the keys. The sound of the piano
clung a while to the dirty wet walls of the street and dissolved into the night. Then he closed the piano lid with
a bang. He was staring away at something. The others followed his gaze. A policeman had just rounded a corner
and was making towards them. His feet moved and his body
seemed to follow.

'Watch it!' whispered the one at the piano. 'I think

it's the one who lives round here and dresses up as a policeman at night and wanders around. He's not a real policeman. He's mad or something. It looks like the one.'

Gonlag and Mason exchanged a glance over the top of the piano. A gust of wind swept down the street, scattering black rain.

When the man who was or was not a policeman came near enough they all stood back from the piano and said with a suspicious kind of politeness, 'Good evening, officer!'

The policeman nodded his helmet and looked at them each briefly, then he did a turn round the piano, even lifting the top and looking inside.

'Hmm,' he said. 'A pianoforte.'

'Yes,' they agreed doubtfully.

'I see,' said the policeman. His uniform certainly looked authentic. He undid the button on his breast pocket and pulled out a shining police whistle. He dangled it on the lanyard, looking at them gravely.

'I could blow it,' he said. 'And I could not.'

The wind blew cold now and the rain spotted their faces. They watched the policeman. He put the whistle back in his pocket, gave the piano one more tour of inspection, said, 'Hey ho!' and walked slowly away. They watched him out of sight.

'Was that the one?' they wanted to know.

But the taller piano-mover wouldn't say. He wasn't sure. But it could have been.

They began to push the piano again, but more slowly now because it was slightly uphill. The noise was as great as ever and Gonlag and Mason started laughing all over again. They had found themselves unexpectedly on the stage, on their own conditions. Enjoying it and laughing. They pushed the piano as fast as they could because it made so much more noise. Although the great excitement of

91

the downhill run was behind them the old piano still maintained a fairly alarming twanging kind of merriment, echoing all the vibrations of the uneven road in its hollow insides. When they paused to take breath they turned, expecting the street behind them to be showing startled bedroom lights and slamming windows, but the street slept on, stirring slightly as the echoes from the piano rocked against the walls and fluttered up into the dome of the night. Far overhead an aeroplane moved. A low rumble heard, a green light visible, and man said to himself, aeroplane, and a pigeon on the roof of the house at the corner of the street looked up and saw nothing but the green light and heard nothing but the dull rumble.

'Not much farther now,' said the shorter piano-mover, the one with the Australian accent. 'Just down the road now and that's it.'

They were beginning to pant and sweat too much and the laughter dried in their mouths. Gonlag thought about the bottle in his pocket and touched it lightly with his free hand. 'All for a corkscrew,' he said to himself. He looked at Mason and saw the sweat shining on his face.

'This is it! Here we are!' said the taller one. 'Now we've got to get it up the stairs to the second floor.'

'What!' said Gonlag and Mason together.

'The second floor,' said the taller one.

Gonlag tapped his pocket and winked at Mason and Mason shrugged.

From the second storey of the house came sounds of revelry and pop music in the right degree to make the eyes of anyone younger than Mason and Gonlag light up and that magic word 'Party' spring to the lips like a call to adventure.

Somehow the four men and the piano managed to move themselves from the street and up the stairs to the second floor. As they had paused at the bottom of the stairs church bells had begun to toll for the midnight Christmas services. And then, as they toiled up the stairs the noise from the party increased so that the impression was one of moving with infinite labour in a small boat from the heavy sea and towards the breaking surf. What lay beyond the surf was never questioned.

And then a tide came, the moon swung, the surf receded, the sea was as bottomless at seven feet as it was at seventy and the struggle for the shore began again.

The noise defined itself to a bright yellow door from behind which more distinct sounds could be heard. A knock, the door opened, and the surf roared. A girl looked them over, recognized the two original piano-movers, admired the piano, said, 'Marvellous Johnno! Do ask your friends in!' The four men and the piano moved soundlessly into the surf, over the threshold, over carpets and into a large darkened room and for a moment the noise stopped and eyes took stock and from the corners of the darkened room came sounds, after the rumbling of the piano and the roaring of the surf, like bats that squeaked and gibbered.

'Come and have a drink,' said the shorter of the two, who was called Johnno. So smacking their hands like good workmen they left the room and went through halls and landings and smaller rooms until they came to the kitchen, round which, it seemed, the party at that moment centred. There was much toasting and Happy Christmassing. Here was the hive and the honey.

From somewhere near a gramophone deafened them with an invitation to make somebody theirs that night. Gonlag nudged Mason and half-drew the bottle from his pocket, thought better of it and pushed it back again. Johnno and the taller piano-mover wormed their way through the mob and came out again carrying bottles of beer and glasses.

'Help yourselves!' they said. 'Stick around, you might have fun, and thanks for helping with the piano.' Then they disappeared.

Gonlag and Mason moved away to a place almost a third of the way along a corridor where it seemed everything was at its noisiest. There they were caught in a vicious crossfire from two gramophones. The corridor was narrow and apart from the dim shapes and harpies in the darkened room all the world seemed to find it necessary to pass them, the more buxom women with a little pleasurable difficulty that neither Gonlag nor Mason tried in any way to diminish. They were all smiles.

'Be all right here for the night,' said Gonlag, following a comely bottom down the passageway with both eyes.

Mason did not answer. He finished his beer and said, 'That was good with the piano, wasn't it?'

Gonlag nodded, wiping his lips. Mason saw the beginning of a wild look in his eyes, as if he were about to cut a leash. 'Come on,' he said, 'we'll get some more booze. I want to get drunk.'

In the ensuing struggle Gonlag came away with a bottle of white wine and a corkscrew and Mason rescued half a bottle of vodka. When they were back in the passageway again Mason said, 'Look, I'm disappearing. I'm going to find a quiet place to drink this. Take a swig before I go.'

'No, thanks,' said Gonlag. 'I think I'll nose around for a while. See you later.'

They parted.

The quiet place that Mason found was the bathroom. When he had shut and locked the door behind him, he sat on the side of the bath and listened to the sounds of the party. Music predominated. There was no sound of the piano. The bathroom became womblike, secluded, white and sane. Now and again came rattles at the doorhandle and impatient, sometimes frantic cries, but Mason heard and was unmoved by them all and soon the strange outer life swept them up and away again. There must have been a lavatory somewhere else.

Mason put a chair under the doorhandle and pushed it firm. He put the plug in the bath, turned on the taps, undressed, sat down in the rising water and put the bottle of vodka in the soap rack. The warm water crept up over his feet and knees and when it was deep enough to lie in, he did so. He reached out for the vodka, unscrewed the cap, and took a good steady swig. White fire leapt down his throat and spread about his body. It was as if he'd swallowed a red ants' nest.

Mason belched hotly.

Someone shook the bathroom door violently and to drown the noise he slid under the water until his ears were covered. Under water all he heard were light and heavy detonations, a sea change. When the detonations stopped he surfaced and took another good mouthful of vodka and let it swill round his mouth and slither round his gullet. The music played as loudly as ever, the stampings to and fro and the shoutings and laughings continued with the same ferocity, but it seemed to Mason that there was a knowledge in it of the balance turned, and the scales weighted in favour of the coming day giving it all a sense of desperation. Inside the bathroom, as an unborn child might guess the coming of the night, Mason felt the far-off dawn.

When half the vodka had gone he took the soap from the rack and washed. He tried standing up in the bath but had difficulty holding his balance. The water turned a thick London grey and he sat up in it like the Phoenix bird, white and glistening. The bath water was getting cold. He took another pull at the vodka and wondered at himself.

He was thin. His ribs showed, one by one. The muscles in his arms looked ludicrously powerful compared to the bony shoulders. The tip of his penis showed pink above the dirty water, like a goldfish coming up for air. He looked at it, hanging his head, laughed aloud and began to finish the bottle.

A new rattling and banging of the door began, interrupting his dreamlike state, sitting there with vodka in his belly, the bottle in his hand and the water going cold around him. There was a particular urgency about this one that kept him from sliding like Leviathan beneath the waters. Instead he listened solemnly to the rattling of the door handle. He noticed with approval that the chair kept its place. He sat in the bath like Solomon at the gates of Heaven.

He spoke at last, surprising himself.

'Come in!' he said.

'I can't, you bloody idiot!' came the reply in low and desperate female tones. 'It's locked.'

Mason liked the voice. Besides the bath water was getting cold. He finished off the vodka with one long swallow, stepped out of the bath, snatched a towel round his hips and opened the door.

A girl moved quickly past him to the washbasin where she was, after a few violent retches, thoroughly sick.

Mason shut the door behind her again and locked it and began to dry himself discreetly, which was difficult. The girl gave a series of dry and unfruitful retches and slumped down on to the lavatory seat beside the washbasin.

'God!' she said. 'Never again.'

Mason quickly put on his pants and his trousers and he began to flap the towel round his torso. But the vodka had hit him and he gave only an impression of a man

96

drying himself, humming quickly between his teeth. When he put his vest and shirt on they clung to his wet skin.

'Don't mind me,' said the girl, looking up.

'All right,' said Mason, and he hummed to himself, 'don't mind me, don't mind me, diddle-iddle-ee.'

She was watching him with weary red eyes.

'This wasn't a fancy-dress party, was it?' she asked, looking him over as he put on his hat and shrugged himself into his overcoat.

'Hard to tell,' said Mason, not understanding her. 'I've been in the bath almost since I got here. I am Solomon at the gate of Heaven. I let you in. You're lucky.' He put hand on hip and did a little dance routine, making great play with his hat.

'You mean Peter,' said the girl. 'Peter's the one.'

'No, I don't,' said Mason. 'And I know because I just said it. Solomon's the man. Sol O Mon. Nomolos. That's the boy.'

The girl looked at the bathwater standing still and scummy in the bath. It was so dirty that an understanding came to her and she said, 'Hadn't you better pull the plug out?'

Mason danced to the bath and did so.

'You must have needed that,' she said.

'What's your name?' asked Mason.

'What's yours?' asked the girl. She had pulled herself together and stood over the washbasin now, swilling her face with cold water.

'Mason,' said Mason.

'All right,' said the girl between the water. 'My name's Watkins.'

'Funny name for a girl,' said Mason.

He handed her a towel and when he saw that she was pretty, his head cleared and he stopped dancing.

'Drink plenty of water now,' he told her.

Watkins obediently did so. She drank four large tumblers, one after the other and when she had done she rubbed her belly and said, 'That's better.'

Someone tried the door and began shouting and banging and demanding to be let in.

Mason reached forward and put his hands over the girl's ears. She did the same to him and they stood there all of a sudden enjoying that kind of slow solemnity that sometimes leads to lovemaking. They kissed and exchanged breath.

When the banging on the door had finished Mason took off his coat and laid the girl on the floor.

'Oh,' she said, 'it's like being reborn. That drink!'

'First the birth struggle,' said Mason.

It was months since he had made love, since he had lain in the liquid anchorage of a woman's thighs. He lingered there. The best of it, he thought, is when your body's doing this and you know there's nothing better it can be doing and you can almost forget about it, and fly. When he was a child he had been able to fly. He had lain face down in bed, taken a deep breath, stood himself on top of the school steps and when he'd got to the bottom he was airborne. If it didn't work he tried again. Then he flew away over hedges and fields and shallow running rivers, and knew what it was to exist in space, to give space a volume and depth, like the deepest ocean.

He thought of the Scarecrow Man and allowed himself to see again what had happened. The scarecrow in the field when he was a boy, the dream, the church-going, and the revelation there. He wondered why it was that only one of the crucifixions in the church had told him that this was the Scarecrow Man and not the one who fat bishops worshipped and whose identity congregations forgot under the mists of rhetoric and incantation thrown over them from the pulpit and choir. He saw again the Scarecrow Man striding beside him as the train sped to London, and how he had vanished as the chimney pots and the advertisements multiplied, as though . . . No. He didn't know why.

'Oooo! Like that!' said the girl. 'Yes! Just like that!'

He wondered where the Scarecrow Man was now and imagined he was everywhere invisible. Perhaps only against green fields and flowers and the old old earth could his radiance be seen. In the towns and cities he went underground. Or like the moon reflected in a pocket mirror, he was only to be seen now and then and only in the right circumstances. He knew he would see the Scarecrow Man again. Just until tomorrow, no, today! And after that he could go back to the country. That was if he wasn't put inside. 'I would like a prison in the country, your worship, if it's all the same to you.' That's what he'd say.

The girl was moaning and shaking her head now and holding him so tightly he was right there with her, nowhere else but lying between her thighs with his lips to her ear, covering her. The girl's excitement caught him up and swept him along until the great cymbals crashed and the heart leapt and the sudden quiet came, and they breathed hard and smiled softly, each to each. Then there was a floor and a bathroom, and a washbasin and footsteps outside the door, and a party in its death throes and a piano doling out the small-hour blues again.

'Watkins,' said Mason. 'I needed to make love to you. You were wonderful.'

'Not Watkins,' said the girl, laughing quietly, 'Bernice, if you please. Do you mind, you've become rather heavy.'

Mason sat back on his heels and looked down at her. 'I'm glad I had a bath,' he said. 'Do you still feel sick?'

'Not at all,' said Bernice. 'I feel marvellous!'

He wondered what else there was to say. There was an

unbroken silence between them which was shattered by another hammering on the door. They both laughed. It was a kind of punctuation. There was more hammering on the door and Gonlag's now drunken voice shouting, 'Come on out of there, Mason! I've been all over the place and that's the only place I haven't looked. Come on out! I've still got the corkscrew!'

'Hold on!' shouted Mason back.

'That's what I'm doing,' said Gonlag more quietly.

As Mason was doing himself up and helping Bernice from the floor, he saw things as they ought to be. Contact, communication, everything shared. It was one of those moments. Rain and thunder did it. Sheltering under shop awnings, waiting for the rain to stop, watching people run for it, listening to the thunder and looking out for the lightning. War did it, sometimes. What else? Love-making too, sometimes, and being drunk. But Mason wasn't content with the exceptional. Sometimes when he was in the country and he looked about him and used his eyes, he would say to himself, now how can I tell that tree there, and that rock, and the old grass, and the whole sweep of that wood, how can I tell it and let it be understood the way it is? Fitting words would come glibly forward and he would try them on. But they all squeaked and pinched here and there, like ill-fitting shoes. What was needed was a word as old as the rock, as green as the grass, as collective as the wood. And always he was driven to sitting down and just saying, that rock there, that clump of grass, that wood; always the particular, because only that was true to what he saw. Words were useless. They were much too general. He wondered about this because communication troubled him and he sometimes imagined a book to himself that had no sentences, but single words. Either the reader knew or he didn't. The communication of visions, that was it!

That was why he hardly ever spoke. He knew the lying ways of truthful words because one day he had seen a tree *as it really was*. It was no longer the tree the farmer saw, nor the tree he saw, nor the tree anyone else in the world saw. It was alone the tree. The particular tree. There was none other like it. It existed alone. Then he blinked and the tree changed in the twinkling of an eye and became again the tree the farmer saw, and he saw and that old woman with the round steel spectacles and the puffy upper lip saw, coming towards him. He had never seen people like that, except the Scarecrow Man. They were different. A tree knew itself.

As he was turning the key in the bathroom door and pulling it open, he saw himself and Gonlag, the Scarecrow Man and Surzo, joining hands together and, then a wave of alcohol blasted around him and Gonlag lurched forward, an unopened bottle in one hand and corkscrew in the other, and he hardly had any time for wondering.

'You've been a long time opening that,' said Mason at once.

'What's that?' said Gonlag. 'Oh, hello, dear, I didn't see you there! I always knew he was wicked.'

The girl came forward and linked her arm in Mason's.

'Hello,' she said, 'another one in fancy-dress.'

'Eh?' said Gonlag. 'Come again?'

'Never mind,' she said.

'This is Bernice,' said Mason to Gonlag. 'We met a little while ago.'

Gonlag became overly polite, put the bottle in his corkscrew hand and reached out to shake hands. Bernice wiggled her hand at him through Mason's arm.

'My name,' said Gonlag, 'is Gonlag,' not letting go of her hand.

'Just Gonlag?' asked Bernice.

101

'I don't see why not,' said Gonlag.

Bernice laughed and said, 'Quite,' rather condescendingly.

'I hope you'll be very happy together,' said Gonlag, 'just what he needs, looking after. Try and get those crazy ideas out of his head and give him some loving.'

'What crazy ideas?' asked Bernice, trying to extricate her hand.

'His Christmas Day ideas. He's going to raid the church.'

'No I'm not,' said Mason.

'Sure he is!' said Gonlag. 'He's going to raid the church and climb up into the pulpit and give them all a blasting!'

'Shut up!' said Mason. 'She . . .'

'Is he really?' asked Bernice excitedly. 'Is it true, Mason?'

'Not the way he says it,' said Mason. 'It's not a stunt.'

'Oh, no?' said Gonlag. 'Tell her about the Scarecrow Man, then!'

'You tell her about Surzo,' said Mason.

Gonlag let go of Bernice's hand and stopped talking.

Someone tried to push past them saying, 'You don't mind if someone else uses the bathroom do you?'

They moved aside and the door slammed.

'Have a drink,' said Gonlag. 'Open the bottle, Mason. We'll all get drunk.'

9

'Do tell me,' said Bernice, 'why both your right hands are covered in white paint and why you both keep your hats on indoors?' There was a discernible cutting edge to her voice.

'Easy,' said Gonlag, pouring out more wine. 'If you haven't got paint brushes, what do you use, and if you don't want to lose your hat where do you put it? I mean this hat of mine's like a roof over my head.'

Mason nodded and Bernice giggled at the explanation.

'You're painters then?' she asked.

'Not really, would you say, Mason?' said Gonlag.

'Certainly not. Though Gonlag's a bit of an artist, one way and another,' said Mason.

'I see,' said Bernice.

The party had receded. The music now being played was quieter, more intimate. The tide had turned, the moon swung and people sat or lay down in the rooms and passage-ways and began to feel their feet again in the ocean. To comfort them in the knowledge that they hadn't reached the shore the spray of the surf flecked their memories still and gave them an easy after-battle languor. There was little laughter. Stale cigarette smoke and over-exposed wine and beer fumes hung in a brown pall about the room. Some-one tiredly played the piano, rolling out the rhythm of the blues. It was Johnno. Everything and everybody lay para-lysed.

Bernice looked from Gonlag to Mason and back again. 'What were you painting?'

'Sorry,' said Gonlag, 'that's our business.'

'All right then,' she said, 'keep it.'

'If I told you we were painting messages from Surzo, you wouldn't be any the wiser would you?' said Gonlag.

'No,' she said, 'who's Surzo?'

'Ah,' said Gonlag, 'you'll have to go to the Royal College of Art and stand outside, to discover that.'

Bernice shook her head, brought out cigarettes and offered them. They smoked in silence, drinking between times. She tried to make a conversation with Mason, but he would hardly reply. Gonlag looked around him.

'Christmas Day!' he said. 'Is this what you call civilization? I wouldn't know. The music and the cigarette butts stuffed into keyholes? You couldn't have this in the jungle, could you?'

'No electricity,' said Mason.

'No electricity,' said Gonlag, and leaning to one side, he spat on the floor.

'Do you mind!' said Bernice outraged.

He and Mason began to laugh. They were sitting on the floor and when they laughed they spilt wine over themselves. Bernice began to laugh too, not wishing, even at that late hour, to have it seem as though they might be laughing at her expense. Her companions had already caused many a raised eyebrow. Johnno sat playing the piano with his back to her, head low over the keys. Poor Johnno, she thought, poor dear Johnno, so eaten up.

Gonlag spat on the floor again, leaning deliberately to one side. 'Any time now, Surzo!' he cried. 'Any time now!'

'Would you mind asking your friend to behave himself?' said Bernice to Mason.

104

'I wouldn't think of doing it,' said Mason. 'He doesn't bother me.'

'Very well then,' she said, 'if it doesn't matter to you how I feel, I'll leave you.'

She got up from the floor steadily enough, crossed the room and walked out of the door.

They watched her go.

'Another drink?' said Gonlag.

'I don't mind,' said Mason.

Gonlag had had the original intention of getting Mason so drunk that night that he would never have been able to get to any church on Christmas Day, morning, noon or night. But intentions like that were unnatural to him and he had soon forgotten all about it. In the end he had had more to drink than Mason probably.

'What makes me laugh,' he said, 'is the whole bloody lot. Honestly. Everything!'

Johnno got up from the piano and left the room.

'After Bernice,' said Gonlag. 'Sticks out a mile. Did you see her looking at him?'

'Silly woman,' said Mason, 'playing her games.'

'I don't know,' said Gonlag, 'I really don't. When I'm sitting it out at Marble Arch I can see it all. As soon as I get up on the stage, you know, and I see things the way other people see them it's all chaos all of a sudden, it's a great big mess. That's when I have to laugh. Still! The piano was good, wasn't it? That was all right!'

Mason laughed to think of it. He could still hear the echo of that journey.

'The play's never been to my liking. It's just a matter of temperament. Except for the odd piano that wants moving. Apart from that I put my feet up in the stalls, boys, and I watch it all going on and what I see makes me spit—there!' and he spat again on the floor. 'It makes me

105

spit and puke and I say to Surzo with my hat in my hand, I say to him, when's it all going to stop, Surzo? And he says, "When de bums is ready, when de bums is good and ready." And sometimes he breathes on the barometer he keeps down there and he sends it shooting high, just to let me know he isn't fooling. That makes me shake in my shoes and sometimes, I've done it once or twice, I've walked around with a board on my back saying, "De joint could blow anytime!"

'It eases me to do that. I'm not on the stage, but I'm sort of selling the ice creams.'

'You ought to try the country,' said Mason. 'It would do you good. You wouldn't want to spit and there's no differences there, it's all one country, it's all the same thing. You want to come. After today, if I'm not put in the jug, I'm away, out of the city.'

The bottle of wine was nearly finished.

'Don't worry,' said Gonlag, 'you won't get nicked or anything,' and he tapped his nose. Then he finished off the the bottle without more ceremony, tilting it up to his lips. 'You don't have to worry about that.'

There was a commotion then outside the door and two broad young men, accompanied by Johnno and Bernice, came into the room. The delegation made straight for where Gonlag and Mason were sitting. Bernice was saying something like, 'perfectly filthy' as they approached.

The larger of the two young men spoke.

'Is it true you've been spitting on the floor of my flat?'

'Ask her,' said Gonlag, nodding towards Bernice.

A voice from the corner of the room said, 'Yes, it's true. He's been doing it ever since he got here.'

Feeling popular support behind him the young man said, 'Well, I think you'd better leave. Johnno said he asked you in but you abused our hospitality. You'll have to go now.'

Gonlag and Mason sat motionless.

'Little puppies,' said Gonlag, winking at Mason and enjoying himself.

The ring of feet around them moved in closer.

After a moment the two men sitting on the floor stood up and faced the young man who was doing the talking with an utter blank indifference. Being so obviously unimpressed made for uneasiness in the circle around them. Feet were shifted. More people came into the room. Johnno, sensing trouble, told Bernice to stand away, but she wouldn't go.

Gonlag was waiting.

'Come on,' said the young man, 'you've had a good time, now it's time to go, so clear off or we'll have to throw you out. It's Christmas and we don't want any trouble.'

'Yes,' said the others, 'clear off!'

Gonlag had heard it. He waited no longer. Mason was all ready to go, pulling at the brim of his hat, when Gonlag put a hand on his arm, staying him.

'Look,' he said, 'it's all right for you. But my mate and I don't know what it is to sleep in a bed. We sleep on the Underground most days and the air there's like it is here, filthy, but you don't have to sleep in it.' He spat on the floor again so deliberately that no one said a word. 'All right,' he said. 'It's Christmas time, you're all having a good time, there's money jingling in your pockets. You eat what you want to, and you drink what you want to. But my mate and I sleep rough every night of the year, we eat what we can pick up off the streets and we don't touch booze from one Christmas to the next. I don't normally talk like this, but now you're going to throw us out, and it's bitter cold outside, I'm going to ask you for a few shillings, a quid or two, to see us over the Christmas.'

Gonlag had spoken almost directly to the leader of the

107

deputation but his words had had their effect on the others. Someone in the passageway outside asked, 'What's going on?' and the answer came, 'A couple of bums making trouble.'

'Well,' said the spokesman, wavering and involuntarily putting his hand in his pocket, and looking around him.

'That's it, sir,' said Gonlag. 'I knew you were a gentleman,' and he took off his hat and held it out. 'What about you others? Give us some money for Christmas, so we can eat. Come on!'

The agony of decision was on every face.

'Then we'll go quietly,' said Gonlag, smiling like a crocodile. 'My nose is broken and I haven't a tooth in my head.'

'Oh, all right,' said the spokesman, who nervously jingled in his pocket and put something in the hat.

'You're a scholar and a gentleman,' said Gonlag, shaking his hat in front of the others. A miraculous tinkling in the gloom followed. He smiled and took his hat into the darker corners of the room. No one talked. Only the money jingled in the bottom of Gonlag's hat, and whenever that happened he said, 'Happy Christmas.'

He toured the room and finally returned to Mason, all eyes upon him. Mason was ready to go and Bernice pressed his hand and held it because her young soul smelt drama and romance and she was moved accordingly. Gonlag backed to the door, beaming, carrying his hat carefully while Mason took a more direct route and waited in the passage for him. When Gonlag was in the doorway he said, 'I hope you all have a very happy Christmas. My mate and I thank you all for your overflowing hospitality.'

They left in silence.

'I like playing the part,' said Gonlag.

The streets were as dark as ever, with no sign of the dawn. A church clock told half past three. They stood under a street-lamp and Gonlag counted the money in his hat and put it into his pocket.

'Seventeen and six,' he declared. 'Not bad.'

'You wouldn't read about it,' said Mason.

They walked away to Marble Arch, avoiding the street down which they had pushed the piano by a tacit understanding.

'You going through with it?' asked Gonlag. 'The church business?'

'Yes,' said Mason.

'But why?' said Gonlag. 'What can you say?'

'I don't know,' said Mason, skipping round a lamp-post, 'but it's like what we wrote on the walls tonight, last night, I've just got to do it. But look, Gonlag, after it's over, why don't you come with me into the country! You'd never think of spitting. There's always somewhere to sleep and an odd job to do. And you might meet the Scarecrow Man too.'

Gonlag scratched his head. The man puzzled him.

'I can't leave Surzo,' he said. 'Who would speak to him? If I wasn't there he might really blow up, and then. . .' He raised his shoulders.

'How do you know Surzo isn't in the country?' said Mason. 'I'll bet you he is. You'll have to dig him out! You'll find him!'

Gonlag considered a while. He had wanted to humour Mason into not going to the church, but he saw it was no use. Perhaps the country wouldn't be too bad at that. And how good to see Surzo walking abroad, perhaps, on a foggy day, down a country lane, blowing on his cigar.

'Well,' he said, 'I might come. See how the mood takes me.'

They were walking down beside Hyde Park, down the Bayswater Road, in the quiet of the night.

'Good,' said Mason.

'What church are you going to anyway?' asked Gonlag innocently.

'That one by Sylvia's, the one that looks like a cinema,' said Mason.

'Oh, I know it,' said Gonlag. So that was the one. All the better, he thought.

The church was mute and stolid. Its form laid no claim to spirituality, as though it had been built in a time of apathy and lifelessness, when God was thundering still in the oak tree and whispering in the olive green of a grass-hopper's leg and saying, 'Where were you when the morning star sang and the suns danced in the heavens?' and no one ever heard. They heard neither the thunder nor the whisper and instead whittled away with the sharp knives of their intellects until they held in their hands a remarkable likeness of themselves and this they placed upon the accepted altar, with suitable reverence, and housed it, very often in a church that looked like a cinema. And the old ones saw and yawned and folded their newspapers and went fast asleep, snoring like pigs. And Surzo was trapped beneath the earth and ceased to stalk the earth in majesty, leaving in the field the Scarecrow Man, arms open, arms embracing, whatever the Lord might bring.

IO

When they reached Marble Arch they found it unusually empty. The women had gone and so had the taxis, one of the hot-dog stalls had disappeared and the remaining one was packing up, though there was a long time to go before the usual commercial dawn. Gonlag hurried forward.

'Two hot dogs,' he said, 'with plenty of onions.'

The two men looked at him.

'You're lashing out, aren't you?' they said.

'Four hot dogs,' said Gonlag.

The two men looked at each other.

'Sure you don't want to buy the stall?' they asked. 'It's going cheap.'

'Six hot dogs,' said Gonlag, 'with plenty of onions.'

The two men grinned at him.

'You've been drinking,' they said. 'Go and join your mates.'

Gonlag took breath, and banged his hard fist on the top of the stall, so that the lids jumped.

'Eight hot dogs,' he said softly, 'with plenty of onions. Eight! And make it quick!'

Mason moved forward and stood by the stall, took his hands from his pockets, and let them hang loosely.

The men behind the stall shrugged. One of them said to the other. 'The gentleman wants some hot dogs, Harry, what are you waiting for?'

'The money,' said Harry.

111

'Drop it,' said his mate. 'Serve the gentleman.'

Harry served up eight hot dogs and plenty of onions. Gonlag paid.

'Happy Christmas,' said the men behind the stall.

'Yes,' said Gonlag.

He and Mason took four each, two in either hand.

'Give them to the blokes along the wall,' said Gonlag, still scowling.

They gave five hot dogs to the huddled forms sitting on the parapet. There were two others. One was fast asleep and the other reeked of methylated spirits. It would have done him no good then. Gonlag ate two and Mason ate one, and they both licked their fingers. Then they rummaged in the waste-paper baskets for newspapers. But there were hardly any there. They did what they could but it was a cold night and they shivered.

The stage was empty. The last hot-dog stall was already trundling away up the Edgware Road, the two men in the shafts eager for a Christmas breakfast. They heard its rumbling echoes lose themselves in the night, and then they were quite alone, the men along the parapet.

Somebody belched, and there was the sound of the licking of fingers. 'Much obliged to you,' said someone, 'Happy Christmas,' said another, 'Yes,' said another, 'Happy Christmas.' And the deep rumbling voice that somehow reminded Gonlag of Surzo said, 'Christ is born!'

The drunk who was drunk on methylated spirits rolled sideways, hit his head on the iron bars, swore, and went to sleep again, slumped on his side. His hat rolled on to the pavement. A hand reached out and put it back on to the drunk's head carefully.

Gonlag made no acknowledgement. He put up his collar and pulled down his hat, 'Easy come, easy go,' he said.

'Thanks for mine,' said Mason. 'It was good.'

'Pity the women are gone,' said Gonlag, 'I'm in a mood to try anything.' He laughed, and spat happily on the pavement. Then he leant back against the railings and went to sleep.

Mason too leant back against the railings and looked up at the sky. He could see no stars. Only the same glow from the city beyond which nothing was visible. He could see nothing. He rubbed his eyes but still no stars were there. He wished very much to be able to see the stars. He felt as though he lived in a terrible prison. The floor of concrete and tarmac, the roof of the rosy lurid impenetrable light, and the walls, the sprawling dimensions of the city. After today, he thought, in just a few more hours, I shall be free of the city. I am a free man but I have this thing to do, and then I'll leave, and perhaps Gonlag will come with me, and the buds will be clinging hard to the branches and the lanes will be muddy and wet and the fields will be blackened stubble and on a grey damp afternoon a blackbird will sing without a care.

Mason waited for the dawn to break and when he saw it well established, he rose to his feet and stretched his limbs. A bird began to sing, Mason couldn't say what kind of bird, and all at once the whole pack of cards fell down and he almost laughed at the concrete and the tarmac and the chimney pots and Battersea Power Station, and at himself for being mastered by them. Instead of laughing, he listened to the bird. The song was moulded before the earth cooled and resolved itself into life and even then, when there was light, it went forward with the light and proclaimed its habitation on the earth. It was Christmas Day!

He looked down at Gonlag's slumped head, and smiled. Then he walked away through the open park gates, through the Park to Notting Hill Gate and the church. As he walked he noticed that crooked trees grow straight. He walked in the path of the bird's song.

Behind on the parapet Gonlag lifted his head cautiously and watched Mason out of sight. Then he too rose and stretched, lifted a hand to one of the other men along the parapet and followed Mason through the Park, trailing him from a distance.

1 1

At the altar a verger in a sweeping black cassock moved
as casually to and fro as a charwoman shaking a duster
from an upstairs window. One by one he lit the candles
there. The flames steadied themselves and burned without
flickering in the airless dusk around the altar. Then he
moved to one side, clicked a switch and the lights went
on all over the church.

When he had nodded to himself, walked through the
choir stalls and past the seats of the clergy and turned
again to bow low to the altar, he saw then, in the now
illumined church, a man sitting halfway up the nave on the
outside seat, wearing a hat. It was as though he had risen
up out of the floor when the lights went on. Christmas Day
that year had begun with a sky of coal and lead and all
over London the lights were on.

The verger couldn't believe his eyes. His quick, light,
vestry-going step faltered and he stopped in mid-stride.

'Have some respect, sir,' he said.

But the man appeared to take no notice, for he sat
motionless as before.

'Have some respect, sir,' said the verger, less emphatically,
walking off to the vestry again, shaking his head.

The verger's words reached Mason indistinctly and were
lost in the dusty crevices of the church. In any case, Mason
sat tight and silent, thinking of nothing, waiting the
moment, while gradually and slowly, in ones and twos and

115

sometimes in whole families the seats filled up around him. The congregation grew. An old woman sat three seats away from him. She had smiled indulgently as she stepped over Mason's boots and now from time to time she glanced sideways at the man with the hat on his head, anxious, as if sitting nearest to him made her the most responsible for the irregularity. Her hand fluttered unwilled to the feathered hat skewered into her hair with a bright and tidy pin. But Mason sat unconscious of everything, staring straight ahead and only dimly aware of the footsteps coming and going and the hushed conversations, of the people waiting the start of the service.

The ten-minute bell tolled. The five-minute bell tolled. Breathless choir boys hurried towards the vestry and disappeared and a man wearing a clerical collar and a shiny grey suit appearing not to hurry at all somehow managed to flit past pillar after pillar towards the same vestry door twice as fast as the choir boys. Up and down the central aisle patrolled three sidesmen, ushering people to their seats with smiles and good wishes, even greeting some by name. Mason could not help being conscious of them. Their neatly-shoed feet paced up and down the aisle, loitering a little, it seemed, whenever they passed his chair. They reminded him of policemen, the bishop's policemen. They had that same officious tread. Their heels rang where other feet pattered.

When the five-minute bell stopped, the congregation had to endure a moment's whispering expectancy and then the vestry door was opened and the verger appeared, carrying a wand in his hand, with the face of a man who knows things are going on behind him. The choir shuffled out after him and then the clergy too, carrying themselves thoughtfully, hands laced around their white surpliced bellies, two of them wearing colourful drapes around their shoulders

116

to indicate they had been to a university and which. With bows to the altar, the procession dispersed to its allotted seats.

'We shall sing,' said an ecclesiastical voice into a microphone, 'Hymn Number Twenty-Eight. Number Twenty-Eight.'

Mason wasn't listening. He noticed the people around him were standing and he stood with them. When they thumbed through their hymn books he opened his and stood with tight lips while verse after verse of the hymn was sung. He was waiting only for the wind to blow, for the leaves to stream and the grasses to bend in the last wind. For he believed he had come to that.

He stood and he sat. He knelt when the others did, at which the old woman sitting near him smiled approvingly. Then it was time for the sermon. Under the cover of more hymn singing the verger led a priest to the foot of the pulpit steps, up which, after bowing low to each other, the priest shuffled through his sermon notes and looked modestly and gravely down the side of the pulpit. He coughed quietly and the loudspeakers sent it booming out above the singing.

The hymn finished. The priest said a short prayer. The congregation mumbled Amen and sat resignedly down.

'First of all,' said the priest, 'may I wish every one of you a most sincerely Happy Christmas,' and he beamed out across the upturned faces and sank back on to his heels. Then he tucked at his surplice and swept the congregation with a more serious glance. In the middle of the nave, instead of an upturned face he saw a down-turned hat. His gaze narrowed on to the hat and he shuffled his notes again unnecessarily.

Mason was unaware of the inspection. He in his turn was looking hard at the smaller pulpit from which the lessons were read and resolution was hardening within him.

'This is the time of year,' said the priest hurriedly, look-

117

ing down at his notes, 'when Christians everywhere, all over the world, of whatever nationality, colour, or denomination, unite and rejoice together and lift their hearts and voices in gratitude for the gift to our poor world of our Saviour Jesus Christ, the Only Begotten Son of God, given by a bountiful and loving God to redeem the sins of our world by His death on the Cross.

'I want to talk to you today about the Message of Christmas, for, as with everything, it behoves us to begin at the beginning and, after rejoicing at Christ's birth, try and understand the final agony of His Ministry here on earth, His Crucifixion, and its relation to our sins and petty quarrels and world-wide wars that tear our world in bloody strife year after year.

'This is the time of year when the family draws its bonds tightly together and sits around the fireside in unity. God's gift to us we echo in presents of our own, and we must think of the whole of Christ's family throughout the world sharing in this spirit of giving and receiving.'

The priest paused and licked his lips, looking up above the congregation and drawing his eyes back towards Mason's hat as a fisherman casts his fly. Then he looked down again at his notes, frowning slightly.

'As we look around the world today, we find, wherever we care to look . . .'

'Wait!' said Mason, standing up from his seat and loudly enough to be heard through the church. 'Wait! The Scarecrow Man! You must tell them about the Scarecrow Man!'

'Wherever we look,' went on the priest, unable to believe his eyes and ears and immediately thinking about the Bishop, 'wherever . . .'

'No!' shouted Mason and walked down the aisle and stood under the pulpit. Looking up at the priest in the pulpit he said, 'There's another one!'

118

The priest's mouth opened and shut but no sound came.

Mason went to the other pulpit. The wind was blowing now, the leaves flew and the trees bowed to the ground and the grasses raced like greyhounds. He climbed the five steps of the pulpit and faced the congregation.

'All I want is for you to know the Scarecrow Man. So you won't ever forget him, when the priests are up there in the pulpit. The Scarecrow Man,' said Mason, 'opening his arms wide . . .'

'Silence!' shouted the priest at him from the pulpit.

But Mason couldn't be silenced, though he could be drowned.

'The Scarecrow Man doesn't want. I don't know who your God is. Crawling sinners! Nonsense! No love there! There's one you'll never hear about in church. Life! If the life goes out of you, the birds come to peck you to pieces and then you're lost!'

The priest in the pulpit turned and motioned to the organist and turned back to the congregation and said loudly, 'We will now all sing Hymn Number Twenty-Six. Rise and sing!'

The congregation straggled to its feet, the organ played and a few loyal voices began to sing, while from the choir the verger and one of the younger priests closed in upon the small pulpit which Mason occupied.

Desperate, Mason began to shout.

'They've got you! They bless your babies and they bless the bombs! Break out! Life's more than they tell you! The Scarecrow Man doesn't . . .'

He was suddenly nearly overbalanced by a hand that had reached up and taken a vicious hold of his ankle. He shook his foot free and tried to go on speaking but the words wouldn't come. The verger and the young priest renewed their attack, climbing up the steps towards him.

119

Mason let fly and kicked the verger in the stomach.

'You swine!' said the young priest quietly.

But they retreated.

The organ swelled, the choir and the congregation straggled along the lines of differing verses and above it Mason shouted, like a battle cry, 'The Scarecrow Man!'

At that moment, at the zenith of confusion, the big main door of the church crashed open and a ragged figure began to make its way down the aisle. The organ played more softly then, the singing withered, and many heads turned at the sound of the crashing of the door.

Without glasses Mason was unable to see the figure was Gonlag. The verger, the young priest, and a sidesman who had come to help, taking advantage of the diversion, closed in upon Mason. The priest in the pulpit watched it all, his knuckles whitening.

Mason was driven back against the side of the pulpit, perching on the edge, ready for flight against the approach of the three men. The verger lunged forward and pushed Mason hard, toppling him backwards over the edge. Cleanly and silently he disappeared. He hit his head on the grey stone flags and broke his neck, and in a second he was dead.

As Mason fell a car passed in the street outside. He looked up and saw a patch of sunlight fallen softly on the stones inside the open church door. Out of the patch of sunlight stood the Scarecrow Man, his arms outstretched, and a robin, Mason could clearly see it, perched on his head, looking about. Mason went to him and the Scarecrow Man said gently, 'Now we'll go to where you wish to be,' and he smiled.

Then Mason's heart leapt within him and he cried aloud, remembering his dream.

And they went away.

The verger, the priest, and the sidesman hurried in panic

down the pulpit steps just as Gonlag, halfway down the aisle, jammed his hat tight on his head and ran fast towards where Mason had fallen. He and the three men reached Mason together.

He was clearly dead. Blood ran thinly from his ears, his head rolled loosely and one leg strayed up the side of the pulpit. An orange had fallen from one of his pockets and rolled a little way.

Gonlag picked up the orange and knelt down to feel Mason's pulse.

'You silly bastard!' he said softly.

He put Mason's head straight and put his hat on his chest. Then he stood up straight and spat hard on the floor of the church.

The verger was blubbering and telling the sidesman, 'I didn't mean him to fall, I didn't.' The priest came down from the pulpit and stood with the others around Mason's body.

'Was he a friend of yours?' he asked Gonlag.

'No,' said Gonlag bitterly. 'Yes.'

'Take the body to the vestry,' directed the priest, 'and phone for the ambulance. This is terrible.'

The verger and the sidesman obeyed.

Gonlag walked away, back down the aisle.

The priest called out to him, 'Where are you going? Who are you? What's your name?' but Gonlag didn't bother to answer or turn around.

As he walked over the threshold of the church he heard the priest saying, 'A terrible thing on Christmas Day. Let us sing that beloved carol, "O come all ye faithful", and commit all to the love of God.'

Gonlag banged the heavy church door behind him and walked down the wide steps to the pavement and the street. Sylvia was waiting for him.

'Well?' she asked.

'He's dead.'

'What!' she said. 'But you only just . . .'

'I was too late.'

'How did it happen?' she asked.

'It doesn't matter how.'

They walked on in silence.

'What about the glasses?' asked Sylvia timidly.

'Give them to me. They're no use now!'

He snatched them from her and threw them onto the pavement, breaking the glass and the frame. He took the orange from his pocket and threw that down too, trying to crush it with his boot. But it rolled into the guttter.

'Look,' he said, 'just leave me alone now. It came off badly. Just leave me alone.'

People walking in Hyde Park that morning to acquire an appetite for the Christmas dinner were surprised to see a red-eyed, hatted, derelict of a man, sitting on a park bench, crying softly and bitterly.

Beneath the pavements and the streets, the sewerage, the gas and water mains, and the electricity, Surzo roared. He roared so loudly that the lightning struck, thinking it had heard thunder.

Gonlag heard too. And he stopped his bitter crying.

'I'll go to the country,' he said.

As he walked along the road to the West he wondered if he might, one day, see Surzo in a country lane, blowing on his cigar and nodding to the trees.

The low clouds had lifted. A dullish light penetrated everywhere, throwing no shadows in the deserted streets.